After several more moments of indulging in their intensely erotic kiss, Micah pulled back. His chest heaved with labored breaths. His eyes were wide with surprise, as if he couldn't yet fully comprehend what had just passed between them.

"Uh, I should…" He pointed toward the elevator.

Bailey nodded. She couldn't speak in coherent sentences either.

Micah gestured to the door of her apartment. "I won't leave until you're safely inside."

Her heart pinched at his compassion. He was such a gentleman.

She took out her key and unlocked the door, then turned back and gave him a wave. It seemed woefully inappropriate after the explosive kiss they'd just shared.

"Good night," she said. "I guess I'll see you later."

Micah nodded. "Good night."

Bailey looked over her shoulder one last time before she entered the apartment. She closed and locked the door behind her, shutting her eyes tight as she banged her head against the wood.

"Should I even ask?"

Her eyes flew open at the sound of her sister's voice. Brianna sat on the couch, her feet tucked underneath her, a sketch pad in her lap.

"I'm in so much trouble," Bailey said.

And it had nothing to do with a crazed kidnapper. This time, she knew exactly what the danger looked like…and how it tasted.

Books by Farrah Rochon

Harlequin Kimani Romance

Huddle with Me Tonight
I'll Catch You
Field of Pleasure
Pleasure Rush
A Forever Kind of Love
Always and Forever
Delectable Desire
Runaway Attraction

FARRAH ROCHON

had dreams of becoming a fashion designer as a teenager, until she discovered she would be expected to wear something other than jeans to work every day. Thankfully, the coffee shop where she writes does not have a dress code.

When Farrah is not penning stories, the avid sports fan feeds her addiction to football by attending New Orleans Saints games.

RUNAWAY
Attraction

FARRAH ROCHON

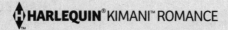
HARLEQUIN® KIMANI™ ROMANCE

For Lauryn and Brandon,
Auntie Farrah loves you!

Every time I think of you, I give thanks to my God.
—Philippians 1:3

Recycling programs
for this product may
not exist in your area.

ISBN-13: 978-0-373-86328-0

RUNAWAY ATTRACTION

Printed in U.S.A.

Dear Reader,

If you take a look at my bio, you'll see that as a teen I had my heart set on becoming a fashion designer. Well, things didn't work out quite the way I planned. I was bitten by the writing bug in college and the rest, as they say, is history.

So you can imagine my elation when I was asked to participate in The Hamiltons: Fashioned with Love continuity series. Through my research for Bailey and Micah's story, I was able to relive some of those long-ago dreams of working in the fashion industry. I discovered that while New York fashion is fun, fast-paced and exciting, I am much better suited to writing about the industry than actually working in it.

I hope you enjoy this glimpse into the thrilling world of New York fashion. Please let me know what you think. You can contact me on Facebook, Twitter or at my website: www.farrahrochon.com.

Happy Reading,

Farrah Rochon

Chapter 1

Bailey Hamilton sat in pensive silence in the backseat of the black Mercedes S600 as it rolled down Columbus Avenue. She practiced the deep-breathing techniques she'd seen a character in a movie use once as a means of calming her nerves. She had no idea if she was doing it correctly. If the butterflies fluttering in her stomach were any indication, that answer was a resounding no.

She clasped her hands together in her lap, trying her best to stop the anxious fidgeting that had plagued her all morning. That wasn't working, either.

The car stopped at a traffic light and a sea of pedestrians flowed past it, all of them going about their day as if this was a normal Tuesday afternoon. For most of them, it probably was. She, on the other hand, had to think long and hard to remember what normal felt like. Her biggest fear over these past few months was that normal was destined to become nothing more than a memory.

I will not let that happen.

Bailey had made that promise to herself before leaving her family-mandated exile in the Virgin Islands last week. She'd existed in a bubble of uncertainty for the past two months. She would not allow another day of her life to be dictated by the actions of the lunatic who'd robbed her of so much already. Today was the first step on the road to normal, and she was more than ready to get there.

Yet with each inch of asphalt the tires traveled, her stomach knotted with growing nerves. She shut her eyes tight behind oversize sunglasses and rested her head against the seat back, apprehension rushing through her despite her efforts to curb it.

She was the one who had insisted on this press conference, which would bring her face-to-face with the media after nearly two months of seclusion. At this point, it was a necessity.

She was fed up with the wild speculations being tossed about by the press, rumors that were becoming more outlandish by the day. The more her family tried to shield her from the outside world, the more rabid the media became. It was time she faced them.

The car pulled into the parking garage on 65th Street underneath Lincoln Center. Bailey's chest grew tight as her heart started the emphatic pounding that signaled a panic attack. She'd learned to recognize the signs over the past couple of months.

Bailey willed herself to calm down, focusing on filling her lungs with deep gulps of air.

"You can do this," she quietly declared.

It had taken a full-fledged campaign to convince her family that she was emotionally strong enough to confront the media. She refused to show even an ounce of weakness. She'd even insisted that the press conference be held at the very site where she had been abducted two months ago, just hours before she was to take to the runway during Fashion Week as the lead model for her family's fashion label, Roger Hamilton Designs.

But as she remained rooted in the backseat of her brother's car, mere yards from that stark basement where she had been found unconscious, Bailey questioned her previous bravado. She should have taken her sister, Brianna's, advice and held the press conference at RHD's studio in SoHo. Maybe facing the press—and her demons at the scene of the crime—was taking on too much, too soon.

"No, you can do this," Bailey reiterated.

"Yes, you can," her brother Daniel said from the front seat.

Bailey's eyes connected with his in the rearview mirror and she smiled. Thank goodness for her family. As much as she begrudged their zealous overprotectiveness, she would not have survived this ordeal without their support.

Bailey sucked in one last cleansing breath as Daniel got out of the car and opened the back door. She clasped the hand he held out to her.

"Look, Bailey." Daniel hesitated, his eyes darting to

the garage's exit. "I meant what I said. You *can* do this. But remember that you don't have to. Just say the word and we're out of here."

"Backing out is not an option." She gave her brother a firm nod. "I'm ready."

"Are you sure?"

"Positive." She squeezed his hand. "I need to do this, Daniel. I'm done hiding. I want to show the world that I'm not broken."

Especially the person who attacked me...who is still out there.

Bailey couldn't ignore the streak of alarm that raced through her body at the thought that her attacker was still at large—and possibly even among the reporters gathered.

Calling on the resilience she used in the cutthroat world of modeling, Bailey put her fear in check and took a moment to check her appearance in the car's gleaming exterior. The pleated chocolate slacks and cream-colored turtleneck underneath her favorite belted, rust-colored peacoat from RHD's fall collection suited her personality much more than the glammed-up fashions she wore when strutting across a runway.

Satisfied with the image reflecting back at her, she turned to her brother.

"Well, let's get this show on the road," she said with an overly bright smile. She could tell by the tension bracketing Daniel's mouth that he saw right through her false optimism.

They started for the plaza at Lincoln Center, where a collection of reporters and cameramen waited. A podium had been set up in front of the fountain, with the Metropolitan Opera House as the backdrop. There was a hum of excited energy buzzing around the courtyard, which only served to ratchet up Bailey's nerves.

Before the incident back in September, she'd thrived on dealing with the press, always ready to flash them a smile as they covered her rise to stardom. But now trepidation pebbled her skin at the sight of them gathered there. She resented the vulnerability the press exposed within her, the outright terror she felt at having to face their questions.

Her entire family stood just to the right of the podium. A lump formed in Bailey's throat at their show of support, ready to act as a wall of defense between her and the media.

Her mother, former fashion model Lila Hamilton, broke away from the pack, striding across the plaza in her signature six-inch heels and a chic cashmere sheath.

"How are you feeling?" her mother asked, rubbing a soothing hand along Bailey's arm. "You don't have to do this, you know," she added, not giving Bailey the chance to answer her question.

"I already tried that," Daniel said. "She's determined."

The concern on her mother's face nearly did Bailey in, but she couldn't allow it to deter her. She gave her a peck on the cheek. "I'll be okay," she reassured both her mother and herself.

Still holding hands, they continued the last few yards to where the others were gathered. Bailey nodded to her father, patriarch of the family and head of Roger Hamilton Designs, who they'd all agreed would be the one to read the prepared statement to the press. He stepped up to the podium, which had at least a dozen microphones attached to it.

"Thank you all for coming," her father began. "The purpose of this press conference is to clear up the misinformation that has flooded the media since Fashion Week. As you all know, my daughter Bailey was meant to be the lead model for Roger Hamilton Designs this year. Due to unforeseen circumstances, she was unable to model during RHD's show. There has been much speculation over the cause of her absence, but I want to assure—"

"Bailey, have you been in rehab?" one reporter called out.

Instant rage flashed across her father's face. Bailey put her hand on his shoulder, halting his retort. "Let me answer them."

"Absolutely not," he said with a firm shake of his head.

"Bailey," her eldest brother, Kyle, warned. She turned to her family, noting the concern on the faces of her mother and her sister, Brianna. Daniel and Kyle both looked as if they would relish doing bodily harm to the reporters.

Bailey turned back to her father. "Remaining silent won't do me any favors. They won't be satisfied until they hear directly from me."

It was more than evident that her father would rather face a den of hungry lions than let her face these reporters, but he reluctantly stepped aside.

Bailey surreptitiously dried her clammy palms on her wool coat before gripping the sides of the podium. Cameras flashed in rapid succession, making her happy that she had kept her sunglasses on. But Bailey refused to hide behind them any longer. She refused to hide behind *anything*.

She took off the sunglasses and placed them on the podium.

"First, I would like to thank you all for coming." Her voice was strong and didn't waver, a mark in the plus column. "When I suggested this press conference, the original plan was to have my father read a prepared statement. But you all are not here to listen to a prepared statement—you're here to ask questions."

The reporters started, but she held both hands up.

"However, let me first say this. I have heard a number of theories about my 'sudden disappearance—'" she made air quotes with her fingers "—during Fashion Week. Everything from entering rehab for drug and alcohol addiction to going to South America for plastic surgery. Let me assure you that I have never used an illegal substance in my life, and the one time I tried to drink anything stronger than champagne I became sick to my stomach."

"What about the plastic surgery?" asked Nathan Porter, a columnist who had covered RHD's fashion shows for years.

It stung that a man she'd known since she was a teenager hanging around the RHD studios had the audacity to ask such a question. She pasted on her most flattering smile as she directed her answer to him.

"Forgive my conceit, Nathan, but there is nothing a plastic surgeon could do to improve this face."

She knew her self-important rejoinder would garner laughs. Bailey had a reputation of being one of the most unpretentious models in the industry. That praise had been delivered by some of the same fashion writers, bloggers and photographers standing before her. These people knew her; they'd helped her get to the brink of superstardom, where she felt herself teetering precariously. She wouldn't go as far as to call them friends, but when you saw the same faces at every fashion event, you couldn't help but form an amiable kinship.

The camaraderie Bailey was feeling dried up with the very next question from a contributor to New York's most popular fashion and beauty blog.

"What about the bag of cocaine that was reportedly found on you the night you disappeared?" the man asked.

"Yes, what about the cocaine, Bailey?"

"How long have you been using?"

"Is it true that you almost overdosed?"

"Why did you stay away for so long?"

"Have you been in rehab?"

The barrage of hostile questions smacked her in the face, causing her to take a step back. Fingers of panic clawed up Bailey's throat with every ugly inquiry hurled her way.

"I…I was suffering from exhaustion," she stammered, using the excuse her family had decided upon while she was hidden away in the Virgin Islands.

"Who's your supplier, Bailey?"

"I don't have a supplier," she said. "I have never used drugs in my life!"

"Then what about the cocaine?" asked the reporter who had initially brought up the drugs. "Where did it come from?"

Her father stepped up to the podium. "We understand that there are still many unanswered questions, but because there is still an ongoing police investigation, we cannot share anything specific about the case. However, I want to stress that Bailey was not involved in any type of criminal activity."

"Do you use the drugs to help you stay so thin?" asked a writer from a major paper, completely ignoring her father's statement.

"Are you being treated for anorexia, Bailey?" another called.

"This press conference is over," her father stated, wrapping his arm around her shoulders and guiding her away from the podium, into the fold of her family, who quickly surrounded her.

Bailey couldn't control the tremors coursing through her body. She knew she should stay and finish the press conference. Walking away now would only feed the frenzy.

But Bailey was too shell-shocked to care, too disoriented by the deluge of antagonistic questions to give a damn that she looked as if she was making a quick escape.

The past ten minutes had served as a reminder that the media was *not* her friend. It didn't matter that some of those writers had been reporting on her family's fashion empire since Bailey was in pigtails. They would turn on her in a hot minute if it meant a juicy headline.

Flanked by her two brothers, Bailey retreated to the parking garage, the sound of the reporters' questions still ringing in her ears as the brisk November air stung her face.

Her entire family had cautioned her against making a public statement so soon after returning to New York. In fact, they'd wanted her to remain in St. Thomas until the person who'd abducted her had been apprehended. After what had just transpired, Bailey was starting to think that maybe she should have listened to them.

"I told you this was a bad idea," Kyle repeated for what seemed like the hundredth time as he paced back and forth, resembling a caged panther.

"Yes, you have." Bailey kneaded the bridge of her nose. "Several times."

Sitting with her legs tucked underneath her on the sofa, she clutched a bronze-colored throw pillow to her chest. The entire family was assembled in the living room of her parents' Central Park West penthouse, in a building her parents co-owned. She and her sister, Brianna, shared an apartment on the tenth floor, and both of her brothers also lived on the premises. However, it was her parents' home that served as the central meeting place when the family got together.

Every person in this room had witnessed her near meltdown after her father had abruptly ended today's ill-advised press conference. The abject shame at not being able to handle the situation caused Bailey to squirm with embarrassment.

For the past hour, her main objective had been figuring out ways to hide just how adversely she'd been affected by today's events. If her family sensed even the slightest indication that her claims of being over the attack were all an act, Bailey knew she would be on a plane back to the Virgin Islands, or to the Swiss Alps or a monastery in Rome. Anywhere but New York, where her abductor was still lurking.

Bailey pulled the pillow tighter to her stomach.

"It was too early for you to put yourself out there like that." Kyle pointed an accusing finger at her. "Those vultures are ruthless."

"Those vultures have been good to RHD in the past," Bailey reminded him. "How many magazine spreads have your designs been featured in?"

"Whatever," her brother said with a derisive snort.

Kyle's fiancée, Zoe Sinclair, caught him by his shirt's hem. Tugging him toward her, Zoe waited until Kyle had seated himself on the arm of her chair before turning to Bailey.

"What's important is whether or not the press conference accomplished what it was intended to accomplish," Zoe said. "Do you think it did that, Bailey?"

"I wanted to show them that I'm not a drug addict strung out on cocaine. Maybe I should have passed out photocopies of my medical records. That's probably the only way they will believe anything I say."

Brianna came into the room carrying the mug of hot tea Bailey had requested, and took the seat next to her.

"Unfortunately, I think today's press conference piqued the media's curiosity more than anything else," Brianna said. "They're going to be more intrusive than ever."

"Should we get a bigger security detail?" Daniel asked.

"No!" Bailey set her tea on the coffee table and stood. "No additional bodyguards. In fact, I don't want any bodyguards at all."

"That's out of the question." Her father, who had been uncharacteristically quiet throughout most of the discussion, stood before the marble fireplace, his arms folded over his chest. "We've had this discussion already, Bailey. The bodyguards remain until whoever assaulted you is taken into custody."

"I can't continue to live like this." She held her hands out, pleading for understanding. "Do any of you know how annoying it is to have someone following your every move? No, you don't. Because all of you are free to go wherever you want without a shadow trailing behind."

"That's because none of us were knocked unconscious by some madman and left for dead," her mother reminded her.

"If whoever attacked me wanted me dead, I wouldn't be alive right now."

Her mother flinched, and Bailey instantly regretted her words, even though she knew she spoke the truth. The reason behind her abduction was as unknown today as it had been when it occurred two months ago, but

Bailey was convinced that her attacker had not wanted her dead.

At least that was what she told herself. The alternative—that her attacker had intended for her to be found not hours but days later—was too upsetting to contemplate.

Bailey covered her face in her hands, pulling in a deep breath. She looked up to find her mother's usually confident brown eyes filled with worry.

"I'm sorry," Bailey said. "But I can't do this anymore. Am I supposed to stay hidden away forever?"

"It's not forever. Just until whoever attacked you is caught," her mother said.

"What if they're never caught?"

A heavy silence fell over the room as her words hung in the air. Bailey's entire being recoiled at the thought of her attacker remaining at large, but it was a real possibility, and every one of them knew it. She forced herself to continue.

"We have to face facts." She took in the stern scowls on her brothers' faces. "It's been two months since the incident. The chances of the police finding the person who did this are slim to none."

"Don't say that." The vehemence in her mother's voice caused Bailey to flinch. But it was spurred by fear, not confidence. "The police are doing everything they can. They are going to arrest whoever did this to you, Bailey."

"I'm sure they will," she said, because that was what her mother needed to hear right now. "But I can't remain in this prison until they're found."

"No one is holding you prisoner," her father insisted. "You can come and go as you please."

"Of course I can, as long as I have an entourage of muscle heads escorting me."

"Hey!" Daniel's brow creased with affront.

Bailey rolled her eyes. "Present company not included."

"Has the media reported anything about the bodyguards?" her father asked, concerned. "We hired that security company because they assured us the bodyguards would be unobtrusive. We don't want anyone knowing that you're under special protection."

"*I* know," Bailey said. "That's what matters."

She could tell by the set of her father's jaw that he wasn't even close to relenting. And when he immediately changed the subject to a national retailer who had approached RHD about launching an affordable clothing line, she knew the matter of bodyguards was now closed.

Bailey refrained from screaming in frustration, but just barely.

She reclaimed her seat on the sofa, listening with half an ear as the rest of her family discussed the possibility of working with the national retailer. At any other time Bailey would have been right in the thick of it, but not today. She had more important things on her mind, namely getting back control of her life.

She'd surrendered the past two months to fear. But if she continued to hide, the person who kidnapped her would win.

That was *not* going to happen.

The best way to reclaim her old life was to get back to doing the things she used to do. She decided to broach an idea she had been mulling over since she'd returned from St. Thomas last week. She waited until the conversation died down before speaking.

"Before you all leave, there's something else I wanted to discuss." Bailey picked up the throw pillow and started fingering the corded edge in an attempt to hide her nerves. "It seems as if the media isn't about to let up any time soon. So I think we should use the publicity to our advantage."

She was faced with a roomful of curious looks.

She set the pillow aside and folded her hands in her lap. Taking a deep breath, Bailey announced, "I think RHD should put on a second fashion show."

There was a beat of silence before Brianna said, "But Fashion Week was just a couple of months ago."

"So? Is there a law that states that we can only hold a show during Fashion Week?" Bailey shrugged. "I know it's one of only a few times a year when all eyes are on the fashion industry, but the downside is that we're competing with every other design house for press. Even though it's not under ideal circumstances, the fact remains that the spotlight is on RHD right now. Why not take advantage of it?"

Her father shook his head. "You've been through enough, Bailey. You need to take it easy."

"I've been taking it easy for two months. If I took it any easier I would be comatose."

Her father frowned and Bailey instantly felt like a petulant child. Considering she had been discovered unconscious and feared dead, she felt even worse. She may have been the one kidnapped, but she wasn't her abductor's only victim. This ordeal had taken a toll on her entire family.

"I'm sorry," she said. "I'm just ready to get back to work." She turned to her sister, whom she could usually count on as an ally. "Think about it, Brianna. This would be the perfect opportunity to reveal the new resort-wear collection." She held her hands out in a plea. "All I ask is that you all at least consider my idea."

She could feel the tension radiating from everyone in the room, but Bailey refused to back down. She *needed* this. She needed to regain the power she'd relinquished to the bastard who'd turned her life upside down. Getting back on the runway was a surefire way to do that.

"Are you sure about this, Bailey?" Kyle asked. "You saw what happened today."

"I'll admit I wasn't prepared for some of the reporters' questions, but a fashion show is my comfort zone. I can handle it." Noncommittal murmurs sounded throughout the room. "Please, just consider it," she practically begged.

With reluctance lacing his words, her father said, "A special event may not be such a bad idea, but the bodyguard stays," he added.

"Dad—"

"It's nonnegotiable, Bailey."

"Dad's right," Daniel said. "You need to have someone with you."

Once again that urge to scream overwhelmed her. She knew her family meant well, but Bailey had never felt more smothered in her entire life, and as the baby of the family, she'd experienced her fair share of smothering. Maybe if she talked to her parents alone, without her siblings offering their two cents, she could get them to budge on their rigid stance.

The conversation soon turned to Kyle and Zoe's wedding, which would be held Thanksgiving weekend. Bailey feigned enthusiasm but her heart wasn't in it. How could she talk about wedding favors and flowers while the rest of her life was mired in uncertainty?

An hour later, back in the apartment she shared with her sister, Bailey grabbed a bottle of Italian spring water from the refrigerator and walked over to her favorite spot in the apartment—the window seat next to a gorgeous view of Central Park.

"Hey," Brianna said from behind her. Bailey jumped so high that water spilled from the bottle. "Sorry. I didn't mean to startle you."

Bailey could lie and say that she had not been startled, but what would be the point? She'd spent the past week doing everything she could to conceal her anxiety from her sister, but Bailey knew Brianna could see right through her.

Mercifully, her sister just put an arm around Bailey and gave her a comforting squeeze. Bailey leaned into the hug, resting her head against Brianna's shoulder.

"I'm proud of what you did today," Brianna said. "I know it wasn't easy."

"No, it wasn't." Bailey blew out a tired breath. "But it was necessary."

"I guess you're right," Brianna said with another re-

assuring squeeze. "The media isn't going to stop hounding you until they're satisfied that they have the full
story."

"Which, if we follow the advice of the detective as-
signed to my case, they will not get until this creep is
caught."

"True, but at least you proved to them that you're
not going to cave under their pressure. That's one good
thing that came out of it." Brianna tilted Bailey's face
up to her. "I just want to make sure you're okay."

"I am," Bailey said, grateful that she didn't choke
on the lie.

She was a lot of things lately, but okay was not one
of them. Flashbacks of being kidnapped assailed her
with increasing frequency, stealing the breath from her
lungs and causing her to break out into cold sweats. It
was *not* a good look for a fashion model.

She had been trying so hard to reclaim her old life,
but how was that even possible when the person who'd
wreaked such havoc was still out there? How would she
ever feel normal again if she was forced to live under
the protection of bodyguards?

Of all the fears her kidnapper had caused, that was
the worst of it—fearing that she would never feel normal again.

Chapter 2

"Hey, Chris, did you find that footage from the Preachers for Prosperity scandal?" Micah Jones focused on his computer screen as he talked to his colleague on speakerphone. "I also need clips of Ezra Singleton's most recent film for tonight's interview."

He lifted the papers scattered around his desk with one hand while he used the other to scroll through the online archives of *The New York Times* as he scanned the results of his most recent search. Micah wanted to double-check the source that would be cited on *Connect,* the hour-long entertainment news program he hosted and produced on New York's WLNY cable channel.

Finding the preproduction checklist he'd been searching for, Micah tore his eyes away from the screen long enough to mark off the tasks he'd already completed.

Scanning the list, he groaned at the amount that still remained. He could forget taking a lunch today.

Despite the mountain of work he faced, he still couldn't shake off his biggest distraction.

His eyes traveled to the second computer monitor that sat at a right angle to his main screen, where Bailey Hamilton's stunning brown eyes stared back at him from yesterday's press conference at Lincoln Center, striking him in the chest with their staggering beauty.

Micah endured the now-familiar response his body produced whenever he saw her, his gut tensing with want. He leaned back in his chair and tilted his head toward the ceiling, his eyes closed tight against the current of desire that charged through his veins. He didn't even try to fight it anymore. It took all he had just to survive the onslaught of need mere thoughts of this woman created within him.

It was probably a good thing he hadn't been among the press conference's invited media. If his body reacted this way to seeing a picture of Bailey, he wasn't sure he trusted himself to be around her in the flesh.

At first, Micah had been upset about having to watch the press conference on TV like the rest of the masses. He understood that he wasn't a member of the press corps that routinely covered New York's fashion scene, but he *had* been the last person to interview Bailey Hamilton before the shit had hit the proverbial fan in September.

And there, no doubt, lay his answer.

Life had not been kind to Roger Hamilton Designs, and to Bailey in particular, since the evening she had been found passed out in a basement in Lincoln Center, allegedly clutching a bag of cocaine. Her family was probably trying to distance her from anything associated with that time period. Unfortunately, that included him.

Micah could only imagine how much it had hurt her not to participate in Fashion Week. He recalled Bailey's excitement during their interview as she'd shared the story of being a little girl in the audience at her very first RHD fashion show, dreaming of one day strolling down the catwalk herself.

She'd brought those dreams to fruition in stunning fashion, becoming one of the most talked about up-and-coming models in the industry. That was why he and the rest of the press had been floored when Bailey had missed RHD's show.

And hours later, when she'd been found with those drugs on her?

Call him a sucker, but Micah refused to believe the rumors running rampant throughout the media and blogosphere. The woman he'd interviewed a few months ago was not a drug addict. He'd seen enough of them in his day to know what a drug addict looked like, even one skilled at hiding their addiction. Something else was going on.

And, like everyone else, Micah wanted to be the one who uncovered the secrets one of New York's biggest names in fashion was hiding.

Shortly after Bailey had been rushed to the hospital, Micah had made a quick visit to his friend Logan Smith, an NYPD detective. He'd tried to get the inside scoop on the Hamilton story, but Logan, as expected, had refused to release specific details. But Micah had been able to tell that there was more to the story. He needed to find out exactly what that *more* was.

And he needed to see her again.

That was what this was really about. He wanted— no, he *needed*—to see Bailey Hamilton again. Like he needed his next damn breath.

Despite her efforts to avoid the paparazzi, she had been photographed and videotaped at least a hundred times since she'd returned to New York last week. But random shots of her getting into cabs or entering RHD wouldn't cut it. Micah needed to see her in the flesh.

He blew out a frustrated sigh as he forced himself to tear his eyes away from her picture. Just then, an instant message popped up on his screen, reminding him that he had a show to produce.

More important, he had an executive producer of local programming job to land.

That was what he should be concentrating on, in-stead of the fashion model who took up way too much of his mental energy. The moment their current EP had announced that he was taking a job at a station in San Francisco, Micah had decided to make his move. Was executive producer a bit lofty for a thirty-year-old? Maybe. But Micah sure as hell wouldn't let that stop him from going for it.

He clicked on the link Chris had provided and down-loaded the video, filing it with the rest of the materials for *Connect*. His show was the highest-rated program in WLNY's prime-time lineup. It was a running joke among his colleagues that the only reason *Connect* pulled such high numbers was because viewers wanted to see Micah's pretty face, but he knew it was all about his guests. He'd been lucky enough to land interviews with some of New York's most popular celebrities.

Tonight he was interviewing Brooklyn-born-and-bred actor Ezra Singleton, who'd made it out of the same housing development where Micah had grown up. Micah sent his production assistant a reminder to have a montage of clips from Ezra's past films ready for the lead-in, and then he printed out the list of questions he'd prepared for tonight's show.

He read the first question three times without comprehending it before tossing the paper aside and pushing away from his desk. How could he concentrate on tonight's interview when the best idea he'd had in his entire career had just popped into his head?

If he wanted to separate himself from his two colleagues who were vying for the executive producer position, he had to stand out from the pack. And he knew just how to do it.

There was one person in New York that *everyone* was trying to land for an exclusive, and he'd had the privilege of being the last person to interview her.

Could he convince Bailey Hamilton to sit down for another interview?

"You can damn sure try," Micah said.

He pulled up Bailey's number, his thumb hovering over it for a few seconds before he tapped the touch screen. Micah attempted to count the loud beat of his pulse pounding in his ears, but it was too rapid to keep up.

After four rings a smooth, feminine "Hello," came across the line.

That voice.

His body reacted just as he'd expected it would.

"Hello, Ms. Hamilton. Bailey," he quickly corrected. She'd given him permission to use her first name during the September interview. He wanted to remind her of that past camaraderie. "This is Micah Jones from WLNY."

"Oh, yes. Hi," she answered.

"Hello," he said again, then winced. For a man who asked questions professionally, his communication skills had plummeted to junior-high-school levels. Micah cleared his throat and tried again.

"I hope I'm not catching you at a bad time. I saw yesterday's press conference. I'm happy to see that you're back in New York and doing well."

"Thank you," she said, then with a humorless laugh added, "Although there are a few people who may argue the point about me doing well. According to some of the comments I've read online, I kept my coat on at yesterday's press conference to hide the track marks on my arms. Never mind the fact that it was thirty degrees out."

"Don't pay attention to that crap. It's garbage."

"And this from a reporter," she said.

"I'm not really a reporter," he reminded her. "At least not in the traditional sense. I produce, direct and interview."

"Mr. Jones, was there something you needed, or did you call to give me your résumé?"

Ouch. Okay, so idle-chitchat time was over.

Her voice hadn't held that edge in September. Micah had no doubts the sharpness in her tone was a direct result of the negative attention that had been heaped upon her and her family these past few months.

"Please, call me Micah," he said. "And, yes, there was a reason behind my call. As a follow-up to the interview we did—"

"I'm not interested in doing one-on-one interviews at this time."

"This wouldn't be an interview," he quickly interjected.

There was a pause. "What are you suggesting exactly?"

What *was* he suggesting? He *did* want a one-on-one. He wanted an exclusive.

"I…I was hoping we could go a step beyond the traditional interview. How do you feel about an hour-long documentary on your life as a model on the cusp of superstardom and a member of New York's first African-American family of fashion?"

Micah had no idea where that had come from, but he had to admit it was pretty good.

"A documentary?" Skepticism practically seeped through the phone line. "I don't think so—"

"Hear me out." He pulled in a fortifying breath and continued. "I understand what you were trying to do with that press conference yesterday."

"I wanted to reconnect with the media after my short hiatus."

"You wanted to quell some of the negative attention that Roger Hamilton Designs has received these past few months." Micah wouldn't let her lie to him or to herself. "I hate to break it to you, Bailey, but you didn't accomplish your goal."

"Oh, thanks." Her flat tone was drenched in annoyance.

"You're fighting an uphill battle. The press doesn't want to hear that you're fine and that everything is business as usual at RHD. The press wants drama."

"What the press wants is to catch me snorting cocaine in some seedy back alley."

"Unfortunately, yes, that's the type of drama many in the press would love."

"And you expect me to agree to give you a full hour of it?"

"No," he stressed. "Look, Bailey, I'm not looking to exploit your situation. And, for the record, I don't believe those drugs were yours."

The line grew so quiet that Micah was afraid the call had dropped.

"What makes you so sure the drugs weren't mine?" she asked. The bite in her tone had lessened.

"Let's just say that I consider myself a good judge of character, and I don't see you as someone who would put your body at risk that way. Give me the chance to show the public the Bailey Hamilton I saw back in September."

"And just who did you see in September?" Not only was there less bite in her tone, but now Bailey actually sounded curious. Micah's heart started to beat a bit faster.

"I saw someone who was driven and motivated and

on top of her game," he answered. "Someone who was considerate, yet commanded the respect of everyone around her. But that's not the person I saw at yesterday's press conference. The person I saw yesterday seemed unsure and completely intimidated."

Micah caught her frustrated groan.

"Take it from someone who's been in the media for a while," he continued. "The more you cower, the less respect they'll give you and the more vicious they'll become. Don't hide from the press anymore, Bailey. I can help you show them that you're back and better than ever."

There was another stretch of silence before she asked, "What's in it for you?"

"What do you mean?"

"Oh, come on. Do you expect me to believe that you want to produce this documentary out of the kindness of your heart, without getting anything in return? Take it from someone who's been in the modeling industry for a while," she said, hurling his words back at him. "The stereotypes are a myth. Fashion model does not equal clueless airhead."

"I don't think you're—"

"Do you know how many requests I've received for interviews since I returned to New York? How much money I've been offered for an exclusive?"

"This isn't just about getting a story out of you, Bailey. Sure, it would be mutually beneficial, but would that be such a bad thing? I'm giving you a chance to tell your story without the media putting some type of salacious spin on it."

"And I'm just supposed to trust that you wouldn't twist the story around to suit your own agenda?"

"That's not the way I operate. You should know that from our previous interview."

"I've learned a lot about how you reporters operate since our previous interview."

Having her systematically lump him in with all other reporters left a bitter taste in Micah's mouth.

"Give me an hour," he said. "One hour. Let me share my vision, and what I believe I can do for both you and RHD."

"I've already witnessed what the media can do for me, and for my family's business. It isn't pretty. Goodbye, Mr. Jones."

Micah met dead air on the other end of the line. He stared at the phone for several moments, disappointment and disbelief ricocheting in his head. He blew out a frustrated breath as he dropped the phone on the desk, trying to think of a way that talking to Bailey Hamilton could have gone any worse.

Bailey braced her hands against the kitchen counter and tried to fight the compulsion to check the window and door locks. She'd done so just a few hours ago. Everything was locked up tight. She was safe.

She squeezed her eyes closed, her arms shaking as she fisted her hands against the cold granite. Pinpricks of unease cascaded down her spine, making her skin crawl. She concentrated on taking deep, measured breaths.

"This is absurd," she whispered.

Unable to fight it a second longer, Bailey pushed away from the counter and raced to the front door. She checked the lock on the knob and the dead bolt. She spent the next ten minutes doing the same on every window in the apartment. She looked in the closets and behind the doors, recognizing that she was being ridiculous, but continuing with her check all the same.

By the time she was done, tears were streaming down her cheeks. The fact that she could not fight the impulse to double-check all of the locks was as scary as the thought of finding one of them unlocked. Bailey knew she was sliding down a slippery slope. She'd told herself that she could handle it, but the more she'd tried to ignore the panic attacks and borderline obsessive behavior, the worse it had become. Maybe once she got back to work, back to *normal,* things would get better.

As she reclaimed her spot on the sofa and tucked her feet underneath her, she picked up her iPhone.

For the past hour she had been vacillating between calling Micah Jones back and apologizing for the curt way she'd ended their call, and just forgetting about him entirely.

That wouldn't happen anytime soon. He wasn't the easily forgotten type.

He also wasn't to blame for the debacle at Lincoln Center, but she had projected her disgust from the fallout of yesterday's press conference onto him. Bailey was beyond frustrated that the conference had done absolutely nothing to curb the relentless speculation by the media; however, the fact that Micah was a member of said media was no excuse for her rudeness. He hadn't asked any of those abrasive questions.

She opened the screen that displayed the most recently received calls, but just as she was about to hit Micah's number, she returned the phone to the coffee table and picked up her iPad instead. Calling him to apologize would only open herself up to more questions. Besides, in his line of work, he was likely on the receiving end of animosity-riddled phone calls on a daily basis.

Bailey returned her attention to the screen in her lap, flipping through the online images from Fashion Week in Paris. Brianna had attended on behalf of RHD, but her sister had been up to more than just representing the family business while visiting the City of Light. She had been falling in love. Bailey was ecstatic that Brianna had found Collin Childs. After the abrupt end of her first marriage, her sister deserved a boost in the romance department.

Brianna would probably say Bailey deserved a boost, too, but romance was the last thing on Bailey's mind. She was far more concerned with getting her life back on track.

Oh, and making sure a crazed kidnapper didn't snatch her again. Yeah, that was pretty important.

She ignored the shudder that ran through her. She was so tired of living in fear, so incredibly frustrated that she couldn't get past it, no matter what methods she tried. The only thing she'd discovered to take her mind off her anxiety was losing herself in work.

Bailey observed the body language of the expressionless models as they towered above the seated audience, commanding the attention of every eye in the room. She had been modeling professionally for ten years now, since she was sixteen years old, but she was always looking for ways to improve her craft.

She tried to concentrate on the images on the screen, but her brain was having none of it. A sickening feeling settled in Bailey's stomach as she set the iPad on the coffee table. What else could she do to convince people that she wasn't some drugged-out fiend?

It wasn't as if she could blame the media for their speculation. She'd been found unconscious with a bag of cocaine in her hands. On the surface it appeared to be the same old story that had been played out countless times before—a model who was caught up in the high life of hard partying. Why should they believe anything she said when she had that kind of evidence against her?

The police department's insistence that her family not share the details of the attack had her hands tied. The only thing she could do was continue to insist that she was the same Bailey Hamilton. If only she could figure out a way to remind the public of the person she had been before her disappearance.

Bailey stopped short. Maybe Micah *could* help.

"No." She shook her head. "It's not a good idea."

She'd just learned firsthand what could happen when the media got too close. She would be crazy to deliberately invite a reporter into her personal space.

But Micah was not like the rest of them. Bailey had sensed that from the minute she'd sat across from him in September. He'd projected a genuineness that had put her at ease. And the documentary he'd suggested was entirely different from her dealings with the media thus far. She could call an end to it if she felt the need. She would be more in control.

She typed "Bailey Hamilton on Connect" into the search box on her iPad. Several clips of the interview popped up in the results.

Her chin in her hand, Bailey watched the interview for the first time. She was never comfortable in interviews, and it showed on her face. The tight lines around her mouth and that fake laugh she'd just given when Micah had asked her about her yoga ritual were both evidence of her nervousness.

She inwardly cringed as she watched herself prattle on about her very first fashion show, but it was Micah's next question and her subsequent answer that caused her entire being to quake with dread. He'd asked about her prerunway ritual. Bailey gripped the iPad in both hands, in shock as she stared at herself talking about her routine of arriving to the show site early so she could perform a walk-through of her runway journey.

"Oh, my God," she said, lifting a shaky hand to cover her mouth.

That was how her attacker had known where to find her. She had just given step-by-step instructions.

"What were you thinking?" she whispered.

She knew what she had *not* been thinking—that someone had been plotting something sinister against her. How could she have known that answering a perfectly innocent question would turn her world upside down?

That was just it—she could not have known. Just as

Micah could not have known that asking such a question would lead to some madman abducting her. She didn't know Micah very well, but Bailey knew he would never have intentionally put her in harm's way.

As she studied his face on the screen, that odd warmth she'd experienced the first time she'd met him crawled its way across her skin. There was no denying that he was handsome, with his medium-brown complexion and those intelligent, intense eyes. She'd felt instantly at ease with him, as if it had been just the two of them enjoying an intimate chat.

It had been easy to let her guard down, and it could have very well been her downfall. She would be smarter the second time around.

Wait. Who said there would be a second time around? She had already decided against doing this documentary. She would be crazy to allow Micah Jones to dig into her life.

Of course, if she dictated what was covered in the documentary, it could be the perfect vehicle to do what she had been trying to do with the press conference yesterday. She could convince everyone that she was still the same Bailey. She could control what was said about her.

She could find a semblance of normal.

Bailey stared at the phone for a moment before picking it up.

"Micah Jones," he answered after the first ring. His voice was solid. Professional. And very, very nice.

Bailey cleared her throat. "Hello again, Mr. Jones. This is Bailey Hamilton."

There was a slight pause, then, "Uh, Bailey. Hi."

She could tell she'd shocked him. A bit of that polish had left his voice.

"I may have been a bit rash during your earlier phone call. I'd like to hear more about this documentary you want to do," she said before she could talk herself out of it. "Are you still interested?"

"Absolutely," he said, the rest of his professionalism going out the window. He sounded as if he'd just won a sweepstakes. "What made you change your mind?"

"I considered what you said, that this would be *my* chance to tell my story."

"There are a lot of people waiting to hear it," he said. His voice had a soothing cadence—he could land a job as a late-night radio host with ease.

"Do you want to meet at RHD's studio?" he asked.

Bailey opened her eyes with a start. She hadn't realized they'd drifted closed.

"Uh, what was that?" she asked.

"I asked if you maybe wanted to meet at RHD. I figure I'll have to sell the idea to your entire family before we can move forward."

She snorted a laugh. "You understand how the Hamilton family operates."

"It's well-known that your family is a close unit, Bailey."

"Yes, that closeness is both a blessing and a curse."

"Really?" She could practically see his quizzical frown. "In what way?"

"Never mind that." She was not in the mood for delving into her family issues, especially with someone she barely knew. "Does tomorrow work for you?"

"Tomorrow is perfect." He paused for a moment. "I have a couple of hours in the afternoon. Can we set up something at one?"

"I can manage that." It wasn't as if she had anything else to do.

"Thanks for agreeing to this, Bailey."

"The only thing I've agreed to do so far is to meet with you," she reminded him.

"Thanks for even that much. This is going to be amazing. I promise you won't regret it."

But as soon as Bailey ended the call, doubts began to swarm her. The last time she'd sat across from Micah Jones for an interview, she'd inadvertently given some lunatic the means with which to abduct her. Was she setting herself up for something even more sinister?

She gripped the sofa's armrest as panic cascaded through her. The all-too-frequent tightness in her chest seized the air in her lungs.

"Stop it," Bailey ordered herself.

She slowly released her grip on the armrest, her chest heaving with her heavy breaths.

She refused to go down this road again today, and she was *not* backing out of this documentary. She needed to regain the power she'd lost—the power that had been stolen from her by a faceless assailant who continued to haunt her.

Not anymore. Micah Jones had just given her a way to take back control of her life. And she was going to use it.

Chapter 3

Bailey spotted Micah as he walked past the coffee shop's large windows and moments later entered through the glass door. He stood at the entrance, his eyes roaming until he spotted her.

A smile broke out across his face, and suddenly an issue she hadn't considered popped into her head. How would she curb the undeniable attraction she'd felt toward him from the moment she'd met him?

The man was the personification of masculine beauty, with dark, intense eyes and chiseled features. His tan suede jacket fit perfectly over his dark brown corduroy pants. He was untying a cream-and-red-plaid scarf from around his neck as he approached the table.

"Hello," he said. "I hope you haven't been waiting long."

"Not at all," Bailey lied. She'd left her apartment over

an hour ago, sneaking away while the bodyguard was in the bathroom. The need to break away from those four walls had all but consumed her.

He nodded toward her half-filled cup. "Do you mind waiting a few minutes while I get coffee?"

"Please, go ahead," she said, gesturing to the counter.

As he studied the menu along the wall behind the baristas, Bailey studied *him*. His broad shoulders filled every inch of his sports coat. His muscular build befitted a professional football player more than a television producer. However, that sculpted jaw and those arresting brown eyes were definitely made for TV.

As she observed him, Bailey concluded that the laid-back, relaxed demeanor that had put her at ease during their interview was not an act. It was evident in the way he walked, the way he stood. He exuded a calmness that made it easy to feel comfortable around him.

That could prove to be dangerous for reasons she hadn't considered when she'd agreed to this meeting. Bailey wasn't oblivious to the tingly sensations that had been traveling along her skin from the second Micah had entered the coffee shop. Those tingles were definitely trouble. She already had too many things to contend with—she had no desire to add a hyperactive libido to her plate.

He returned to the table with a paper coffee cup and took the seat across from her.

"Thanks again for agreeing to meet with me," he said. "I have to give you fair warning—I'm going to do everything I can to convince you to sign on for this project. I really think this documentary will be amazing, Bailey. Not just amazing, but beneficial, too."

"Why don't you tell me exactly what the documentary will entail? But, first, here's *my* fair warning—I am not doing another live, one-on-one interview on your show. On anyone's show, for that matter. I know better than to expose myself to that kind of ridicule."

His brow wrinkled, drawing her attention to the deep brown of his irises. They were so dark they were almost black, and they had the frightening ability to steal the breath from her lungs.

"What makes you think you would be ridiculed on my show?" he asked. "Did I give you reason to believe that any moment of our previous interview wasn't one-hundred-percent genuine?"

"No, but as I told you yesterday, things have changed significantly since our first interview. You did see the press conference, didn't you?"

"I would never treat you that way."

"Why should I believe that? You're a reporter—"

"I'm not—"

"Fine," she said with an impatient flick of her wrist. "Producer, TV personality, whatever you want to call yourself. The point is that it's your job to get the dirt on people. And no matter how much I tell everyone that there isn't any real dirt out there about me, the media doesn't seem to comprehend that. Some of them have taken to actually making stuff up. My brother thinks I should file a slander lawsuit."

"Filing a lawsuit will only draw more attention to yourself, which those same reporters will no doubt put a negative spin on." He folded his hands on the table and leaned forward. In a slightly lower and devastatingly smooth voice he said, "Look, Bailey. I know you've had a contentious relationship with the media lately, but you don't have to worry about me twisting the story for my own benefit. That's not how I operate. I make sure everything I say on *Connect* is thoroughly vetted."

"I don't care how thorough you are. Just know that I am not joining you on your couch again." His brow quirked and an immediate rush of heat flooded her face. "You know what I mean," she said.

His lips curved in a quick, sexy grin as he reached for his coffee.

"I do," he said after taking a sip. "But it doesn't matter, because what I have in mind doesn't involve you on my couch."

Bailey bit her bottom lip to stop herself from laughing. This volleying of sexual innuendo was totally inappropriate given how much was at stake.

She cleared her throat and sat up straighter. "What exactly *do* you have in mind?"

His brow cocked again.

"In regards to the documentary," Bailey clarified. Lord, she *so* did not have the mental energy to engage in suggestive banter with Micah Jones.

He set his cup aside and folded his hands on the table. "Before you even ask, I'm not seeking to do an exposé or some other such nonsense that would harm your reputation rather than help it."

"Exactly what did I do to warrant this sudden concern for my reputation? Especially from a reporter?"

His long-suffering sigh was genuine, and Bailey realized in that moment that the sarcasm toward him was completely unwarranted. Micah had never been anything but honest and sincere, both during their interview and since he'd contacted her yesterday. Yet she'd mentally lumped him in with the rest of the paparazzi who'd set out to make her life a living hell.

"I'm sorry," she said. "Blame my bitchiness on lack of sleep and an abundance of stress."

"The last thing I want to do is stress you out. My goal is to give New Yorkers a more in-depth look into your life from *your* perspective. And you were right when you said that I would get something out of it, too. Your interview was one of the highest rated in *Connect*'s history. The numbers guys back at the network think it was because of you and your appeal, or the hype that was surrounding Fashion Week at the time, or the attraction of RHD as a company—no one can really pinpoint it. But personally, I think you were the biggest draw."

"Me?"

"Yes, Bailey. You were fascinating. You came across as the glamorous supermodel you are, but you were so down-to-earth and approachable. You were completely different from what I'd expected."

She put her elbow on the table and cradled her chin in her palm. "Exactly what did you expect?"

"A diva," he answered. "But you weren't. You were so…authentic."

A smile lifted the corner of her mouth. "Funny you should use that word. My brother Daniel came up with RHD's slogan: Authentic Fashion."

"It's more than just a slogan—it's how you really are. I sensed that from the moment I met you, and that's what I want to show the rest of the world. I want to give our viewers a glimpse into what it's really like to be Bailey Hamilton."

That was easy. Confused. Afraid. Going out of her mind.

No. That was *not* who she was, and that was not what she wanted the world to see. It was not what she wanted Micah to see, either. Hearing him recount her attributes in such a flattering way had summoned those tingles again.

With a self-deprecating chuckle, Bailey asked, "Do you really think people want to know that the real Bailey Hamilton would rather lounge around in sweatpants and an old T-shirt instead of those runway-ready outfits I normally wear in public?"

"You're the only woman I know who can make sweatpants and a T-shirt look like something that belongs on a runway."

Maybe those words wouldn't have set the butterflies in her stomach aflutter if he hadn't spoken them in such a soft, seductive voice. Their eyes connected, and Bailey was instantly entrapped by the heat radiating from him. They stared at each other much too long to deny what had passed between them. Bailey was the first to look away.

She peered up at a framed black-and-white photo of a coffee cup on the wall next to them.

"So," she said, after she was able to get the air flowing into her lungs again, "I'm assuming this documentary is going to be about more than just the clothes I wear?"

She returned her gaze to Micah to find him still staring at her with that bold, penetrating look. Desire flared to life within her, and Bailey had to pull in another deep breath.

"Micah, I can't," she whispered. She couldn't handle this right now. She had too much on her plate; she couldn't heap on this dose of outrageously intense attraction.

"I know," he said.

The air continued to pulse with deep, dark need. The fervency of it was palpable, the electricity arcing across the table undeniable. But deny it she would.

"The documentary," Bailey prompted.

"Yes." Micah cleared his throat as he picked up his phone and swiped across the touch screen. "I've been brainstorming. I want to give my viewers an inside look into RHD and the modeling industry as seen through your eyes. I want you to tell the story, Bailey."

"Why me?" she asked. "I'm not the only one who can give an insider's look into the industry."

"You're the one everyone wants," he said.

It was on the tip of her tongue to ask if he included himself among that number, but that would require a level of boldness she'd never felt off the runway. Instead, Bailey took a healthy sip of her tea to give herself something to do while she processed his words—and avoid the penetrating look that had returned to his eyes.

He propped his elbows on the table and folded his

hands, resting his forehead on them for a moment before looking up at her.

"Okay, can we just get this out in the open?" He blew out a deep breath. "I'm attracted to you. I have been from the very beginning."

A dizzying jolt of awareness raced through her at his announcement. Before she could respond, he held both hands up. "But that's not the reason I want to do this documentary. In fact, it will make things harder."

Bailey couldn't help the laugh that sprung from her mouth.

His brow dipped in a frown seconds before he caught his unintended double entendre. "You know what I mean," Micah said.

"I do. I'm attract—"

Micah stopped her with a hard shake of his head. "Don't tell me the attraction is mutual. That's not what I need to hear right now." He ran a hand down his face, the picture of barely contained sexual frustration. "Look, Bailey, I need you to be the subject of this documentary and nothing more. I'd give my left arm to have you be more, but it wouldn't be a good idea—not if we're going to work together."

Bailey knew that what he suggested was the best thing for both of them, but that didn't stop her from feeling a little hurt. She pushed the hurt to the side.

She was carrying a boatload of baggage; she didn't need to add any romantic entanglements. She had a specific goal in mind when it came to this documentary, and she needed to remember that.

"I agree," she answered. "We need to keep this on a strictly professional playing field."

Micah's shoulders relaxed, but his expression still held traces of longing and regret.

Bailey could commiserate.

"So," he asked, "have I convinced you that this documentary is the best idea in the history of the world yet?"

"Maybe." She laughed. "But unfortunately for you, I'm not the only one you have to convince."

"Ah, yes." He sat back in his chair and rubbed a hand along the back of his neck. "The package deal that is the Hamilton family."

"I know, I know. We're obnoxiously close-knit."

His head tipped to the side and he gave her a curious stare. "You say that as if it's a bad thing."

Bailey lifted her shoulders in a light shrug as she wrapped her palms around her tea. "I complain, but it's not all bad. Being the baby of the family, I'm spoiled by everyone, and I take full advantage of it whenever I can."

She laughed, but he didn't join in. His body stiffened as he looked past her.

"Bailey, I don't want to alarm you, but there's this guy on the other side of the coffee shop who walked in about ten minutes ago, and he's been staring at you ever since."

Bailey glanced over her shoulder and cringed under her bodyguard's reprimanding gaze.

"Oh, great," she muttered, feeling like a teenager who'd been caught sneaking out of the house. She pivoted toward Nick, one of the three bodyguards who took turns watching her every single move.

She put a finger up to tell Nick she needed more time. Then she turned back to Micah and said, "Don't ask."

"You don't have to answer, but I *have* to ask."

Of course he did. Regardless of whatever label he tried to put on it, he *was* a reporter. It was in his nature to ask.

"He's…a bodyguard," she said.

Micah's gaze went from curious to concerned.

She shook her head. "I can't get into it, so please, don't ask. Just pretend you didn't see him. No, wait!" She stopped short, realizing this could very well work in her favor. "When you meet with my family, let that be the first thing you bring up. Maybe then my dad will see just how ridiculous it is to have these bodyguards following me around."

Micah's brow furrowed. When he spoke, his voice was softer. "Bailey, what really happened during Fashion Week? I'm not buying this exhaustion story your family has been feeding to the press. You were so excited about RHD's show you could hardly sit still during our interview, yet you pull out right before your big moment? It doesn't take a rocket scientist to realize that there's more to the story. What happened to you that night?"

"You said you wouldn't grill me like a reporter."

"This isn't me being a reporter. This is me—" he tapped his fingers to his chest "—being concerned about you. I just want to know that you're okay."

She tilted her head to the side. "Why?" she asked,

although she already had her answer. The intensity in his eyes suggested that his question was wrapped in something much more powerful than just concern, and Bailey suddenly realized that trying to fight the pull between them would be a thousand times harder than she'd imagined.

The attraction had sparked the moment she'd sat across from him a few months ago. She had tried to write it off as insignificant. But there was nothing insignificant about the heat she could feel like a physical touch on her skin right now.

Micah reached across the table. "Bailey," he said, but then his cell phone rang, making them both jump. He pulled his hand back.

A breath she didn't realize she was holding rushed out of her mouth.

He answered the phone, and Bailey could tell by the look on his face that he wasn't thrilled with whatever the person on the other end of the line was telling him. He disconnected the call and grimaced.

"We're going to have to cut our meeting short," he said. "I need to get back down to the station."

"That's fine," she said, even as a flicker of despondency in her chest contradicted her words. Bailey ignored the unwarranted emotion. "So when do you want to meet at RHD?"

"The sooner, the better. We're meeting about our production schedule this afternoon, so I'll have an idea of a target airdate for the documentary before I meet with your family."

"Why don't you make sure there's a definite airdate before we bring my family into this?"

"I think we'll be able to convince them," he said.

Her brow hitched. "We? So we're a team now?"

"I'd like to think so." Did his voice deepen, or was her mind teasing her? "When it comes to the documentary, we have the same goal in mind," he finished.

"We both have goals in mind, but I'm not convinced they're the same," Bailey said. "Regardless, the documentary will be mutually beneficial. But I have to warn you, Micah—convincing my family won't be easy."

The smile that drew up the corner of his mouth was so tempting Bailey could hardly stand it. "Well, it seems as if we've got our work cut out for us," he said with a wink. "I'll see you later."

He stood and nodded at Nick as he walked out of the coffee shop.

"Stop hovering," Brianna demanded as she sketched at her worktable.

"I'm not hovering," Bailey defended. "I'm just… perusing."

"Since when do you peruse?" Brianna smeared gray charcoal, filling in a drawing of a wrap dress. She covered her mouth and nose with her other hand. "Get away," she said. "That perfume is making me want to hurl."

Bailey laughed. "It's your scent." She sniffed her wrist, where she'd dabbed the citrus, jasmine and patchouli perfume Brianna had created for the launch of her new clothing line.

Brianna set her pencil on the desk and spun her stool around. "Okay, what's going on with you?"

Bailey's throat closed up with panic as she waited for her sister to ask why she was holding clandestine meetings with a television personality, but Brianna didn't mention anything. Apparently, Nick had kept his word. Whether he'd done so because she'd asked him to or because he was afraid he would get in trouble for allowing his charge to get away, Bailey wasn't sure. She was just grateful that she didn't have her entire family raining fury down on her head about how foolish it had been to sneak away.

However, they would all find out soon enough. Which was why she needed her sister.

"First, don't be mad," Bailey started.

Brianna's eyes closed. "What did you do?"

"I met with Micah Jones today. You know, the guy who interviewed me a few months ago."

"I know who Micah Jones is," Brianna said. "But why in heaven's name are you meeting with him? Bailey, you need to steer clear of the press until all of this blows over."

"Do you really think this will all just blow over, Brianna? Be real. Weren't you the one who said that the media isn't going to back down?"

"That doesn't mean you should purposely walk into the lion's den."

"I wouldn't call him a lion," Bailey argued. When Brianna's eyes narrowed, she instantly realized it was the wrong thing to say. It was her sister, after all, who had mentioned noticing a spark between Micah and Bailey during the interview. She didn't give Brianna a chance to bring it up.

"Look," Bailey continued, "that press conference revealed a lot of things—mainly that the press plans to pursue any story they can come up with regarding my disappearance. They are willing to say whatever they think will sell."

"So how does meeting with Micah Jones—who is media, I might add—change any of that?"

Her sister was making the same arguments Bailey had made herself, but after speaking with Micah, she was no longer willing to lump him in with the rest of those reporters. He was different.

And she needed an ally, someone in the media whom she could trust not to take advantage of her. Something in her gut told her she could trust Micah. All she had to do was convince her family.

Oh, and fight off her skin-tingling attraction to him. Yeah, that would make things a *lot* easier.

"I'm not naive enough to think that the rumors will go away," Bailey told her sister. "But if I agree to give Micah exclusive access, I can reach the public in a more controlled way."

Brianna folded her arms, her brow forming an inquisitive peak. "What type of exclusive access are you thinking about giving him?"

Bailey felt her face flush. "It's not what you're thinking, so don't even go there."

"If you want to tell yourself that, be my guest. But

you know that I can read you like a bedtime story, and I saw the way the two of you interacted during that interview. I'm pretty sure the only thing that prevented you from jumping him on his couch was the fact that Mom and Dad were watching."

"Brianna!" Embarrassment scorched her cheeks, but Bailey continued on. "He wants to do more than just an interview—he wants to shoot a documentary. I think this could be a really good thing, Brianna."

"It sounds to me as if you've already made up your mind."

"As if that matters. Every decision about my life these days is made by a committee. Daniel and Kyle both think the press conference was a disaster. And if Dad had his way, I would be locked in some safe house for the foreseeable future."

"Bailey, be reasonable. No one is intentionally trying to make your life a living hell. This is about your safety." Brianna captured Bailey's hands between her palms and rubbed them. "Do you know how terrifying it was when you went missing? For a while there, I would have voted for the safe house, too."

Not for the first time during this ordeal, Bailey felt like a sulky teenager. She had to remind herself to cut her family some slack. When she put herself in their shoes, she could understand their overprotectiveness.

"I'm sorry," she told her sister. "If this had happened to you, I would probably feel the same way."

Brianna wrapped her arm around Bailey's shoulder and leaned her head against her temple. "I know the bodyguards and constant hovering aren't ideal, but there is still someone out there who hurt you, Bailey."

As if she could forget. As if she didn't wake up with night sweats, her body frozen in fear at the thought of the person who'd abducted her just waiting for the chance to finish what he'd started.

But she refused to succumb to that fear any longer.

"If I continue to stay hidden away like this, my kidnapper wins, Brianna. I can't let him win."

Her sister's understanding gaze pulled at Bailey's heart.

"I know," she said, running a soothing hand down Bailey's arm. "And he won't. This will all be over soon. We have to believe that the police will get a break in the case, and we can finally put this to rest."

"And, in the meantime, maybe allowing Micah full access wouldn't be such a bad thing," Bailey said. "It wouldn't be like a live interview where he could catch me in a trick question. I would be in control."

"That's true." Brianna slowly nodded. "So what's my role in this?"

"A united front would make it easier to convince Dad."

"Since when?" her sister asked. "You know once he makes up his mind even an act of Congress can't change it. If he's against this, nothing you, me or Micah Jones says will matter."

"I have to try," Bailey said. "I'm going crazy just sitting around waiting for something good to happen. I want to *make* it happen."

"Well, I'm here for you if you need me."

"Thank you," Bailey said, pulling her in for a hug.

Brianna gave her a sad smile. "Good luck convincing the rest of the family to go along with this. You'll need it."

Chapter 4

Micah stood just outside the doors of the RHD studio. The heart and soul of the multimillion-dollar empire was housed in a five-story cast-iron building in SoHo, similar to many of the grand structures in the historic neighborhood.

Micah hoisted his leather messenger bag more securely onto his shoulder and entered the building. A receptionist dressed casually in jeans and a sweater greeted him.

"Micah Jones, here to meet with Bailey Hamilton," he said.

Several moments later, Micah was allowed to enter the inner sanctum of RHD.

It was pretty much what he'd imagined a fashion studio to look like: a huge open space with yards of fabric draped across polished wooden tables. Headless mannequins stood in various states of undress, and caged light fixtures hung from the high ceilings.

The mood, however, was nothing like he'd imagined. Micah had pictured high-strung designers frantically running around, yelling demands to their minions. Basically, the stuff he'd seen on television.

Instead, the atmosphere was calm and relatively quiet. Several people worked at computer monitors. Most were wearing earphones, their heads bobbing to music.

"Micah?"

He turned at the cool voice that called his name. His breath hitched at the sight of Bailey. It was the same reaction he'd experienced yesterday when they'd met at the coffee shop. Hell, it was the same reaction he had whenever he just *thought* about her.

She was ten times more beautiful in the flesh than she was on television and in magazines, with her high cheekbones and those exotic eyes. There was this sense of unpretentiousness about her in person that didn't come through in photos, a realness that had struck Micah from the moment she'd walked onto the set of *Connect*.

For the barest moment, he allowed himself to indulge in the fantasy of being more than just a professional acquaintance. God, what he wouldn't give to be more than that to her.

Her vivid eyes were glittering with a mixture of anticipation and nervousness. "So are you sure you're ready for this?"

His brows arched. "You make it sound as if I should be afraid."

"Possibly. My dad is pretty good at keeping his cool, but Mom can turn into a grizzly bear when it comes to her kids."

He chuckled. "I've got myself an overprotective mama bear, too. Wouldn't trade her for the world."

Bailey led him down a corridor and into an elevator. Micah stared up at the numbers as they ascended, feeling as if he was going to burst out of his skin. For several weeks after he'd first interviewed her, he'd wondered if his attraction to Bailey had really been as intense as he'd remembered. Standing beside her right now, breathing in her clean, delicate scent, Micah had all the proof he needed.

Attraction didn't even come close. There wasn't a word in the English language that could fully describe what he felt toward this woman.

Working on this project with her would be hell. Pure, unadulterated, lust-drenched hell.

On the bright side, with all the cold showers in his future, at least his utility bill wouldn't be much this winter.

The elevator stopped on the fifth floor. They stepped out of the car and walked straight ahead to a set of double doors.

He followed Bailey into her father's office, which was smaller than Micah had anticipated. Although, to be honest, the unpretentiousness of the entire place surprised him. RHD was outstandingly successful, but their headquarters were impressively low-key. Micah took note.

On the walls of the neat office were framed photographs of what he could only assume were RHD fashions through the years. Micah recognized a younger Lila Hamilton in the photo mounted directly above Roger Hamilton's desk. She had been a knockout. Actually, she still was. Like mother, like daughter.

"Good afternoon," Micah greeted.

"Good afternoon," Roger Hamilton said. He came around the desk and shook Micah's hand. Then he motioned to the sitting area on the other side of the office, which contained a love seat, two armchairs and a coffee table.

"If you give us just a minute, my wife will be—"

"I'm here," Lila Hamilton said as she entered the office, closing the door behind her. She shook Micah's hand and sat on the love seat. She patted the seat next to her, motioning for Bailey to join her.

Micah sat in the armchair across from Roger, and they quickly got down to business.

"What exactly is it that you're looking to do with this documentary, Mr. Jones?" Lila Hamilton asked.

"My goal is to show Bailey in her natural element, and also show how RHD has influenced her life. The overwhelming media attention she's received in the past few months has proved that Bailey is in high demand. Her interview on *Connect* was one of the highest rated in the show's history. People want to know about her."

"It seems as if people want to believe the very worst about Bailey," Lila said.

"Exactly. They don't care about the truth," Roger

added. "That press conference only added fuel to the fire."

"The speculation won't stop if we do nothing," Bailey pointed out.

"Bailey's right. The only way to put a stop to these rumors is to face them head-on. What better way to do that than to show the world that Bailey isn't what so many in the media are saying she is?"

"And why would people believe what's said in this documentary when they wouldn't believe what she said during the press conference?"

"It's my job to make them believe it, and, pardon my language, but I'm damn good at my job," Micah said. "My goal is to convince the public to believe what I discovered when I began my research before Bailey's first appearance on *Connect*—that RHD really is a family business that has stayed true to its roots. It's rare to see a family as interconnected as yours that still manages to stay on top of their game."

"So will the documentary be on Bailey, or Roger Hamilton Designs?" Lila Hamilton asked.

"A little of both, but I want the main focus to be on Bailey for two reasons. First, in my view, this is a continuation of our interview. Second—and I mean no disrespect to anyone else in the family—Bailey is a fascinating subject. She's the one everyone sees. The working title is *Bailey Hamilton: The Face of a Franchise.* There is a lot of pressure in that role, but from what I've gathered, your daughter has shouldered it with unbelievable grace, despite everything that she's been through these past couple of months."

Micah chanced a look at Bailey. Her luminous eyes were focused on him, but unreadable. He forced himself to return his attention to Roger.

"I want to film Bailey here at the studio, shopping, hanging out with her friends and, once she's returned, on the runway."

"I don't want Bailey mixed up in some sleazy reality-TV show," Roger said.

"No, no, no." Micah held both palms up. "I have no intentions of exploiting your daughter. That's a promise."

Roger tapped his lips with a capped ink pen. He turned to Bailey.

"Are you really up for something like this?"

"Absolutely." Bailey straightened in her chair. "I need to get back to work, Dad. And just think about the good publicity this will bring to RHD."

"I'm not concerned about the business right now. I want to make sure you can handle someone intruding on your life, Bailey."

"I can handle it," she said. "But I want Daniel to be part of it."

Micah whipped his head around. "What?"

"I want my brother to be part of the production," she said. "Daniel is in charge of RHD's marketing. He's a genius behind the camera."

So is any fool with a phone these days, Micah nearly blurted out.

He shook his head. "I'm not sure about bringing an outsider into my team."

"If you want to shoot this documentary, you'll figure out a way to make it happen."

She was resolute, and Micah had to admit her take-charge attitude was sexy as hell. Too bad he was completely against what she was proposing.

"I would feel a lot better about Bailey participating if Daniel were there to protect her," Lila said.

"I don't want Daniel there as a bodyguard," Bailey told her mother. "I want him there because he is a creative genius and I value his input." She turned to Micah. "So what will it be?"

Damn it. This was a wrinkle he hadn't anticipated.

Not only was he not convinced that he could get the powers that be at WLNY to allow Daniel to come on board, but Micah wasn't so sure he wanted him involved, either. This documentary was his ticket to that executive producer position. He didn't want any asterisk in the mix, and giving up some control over production to Daniel Hamilton could turn into a really huge asterisk. This was *his* project.

But if it meant not getting the exclusive on Bailey at all, it was a moot point. He would do whatever he had to do to secure her participation.

"Okay," he said. "I think we can make that happen."

Roger Hamilton looked pointedly at his daughter. "Are you sure you're up for this, Bailey?"

"If Daniel can be part of it, then yes," she answered.

There was a pregnant pause. Roger Hamilton looked from his wife to Bailey and then to Micah. Almost instantly the tension in the room ratcheted up several notches.

Roger blew out a weary breath. "Well, if this documentary is really going to happen, I think Mr. Jones needs to know the entire story." The man's grave voice caused the hair to rise up on the back of Micah's neck.

"Story?" Micah glanced at Bailey's mother. Stress lines had formed around her mouth. "What story?" he asked.

Roger tossed the pen he'd been holding onto the coffee table and folded his hands in front of him. "No doubt you've heard the rumors that Bailey was found unconscious with a bag of cocaine during Fashion Week."

"It's been all over the press ever since," Micah pointed out.

"The cocaine was not mine," Bailey said. "Someone planted it on me. And I didn't skip out on the RHD show." She sucked in a deep breath and let it out slowly before saying, "I was kidnapped."

Micah's blood chilled in his veins. "How?" was the only word he managed to get out.

"Someone grabbed me after my prerunway ritual. I'm still not completely sure how it all happened. Memories have been coming back to me in small doses." She pulled in another breath and continued, her voice shakier than it had been just moments ago. "I remember doing my normal walk-through and then returning to the dressing room. The next thing I knew, I was waking up in the hospital."

Bone-aching fear seeped through him.

"And no one—" Micah had to take a moment to clear the unease clogging his throat. "And no one saw anything?"

Bailey shook her head. "I prefer to do my prerunway ritual when there's no one there to disturb me."

He nodded. "I remember you talking about the routine during our interview."

The moment he said the words, fingers of dread scraped down Micah's spine. *He* was the one who'd pressed her to talk about the special routine she performed before every fashion show.

He'd practically handed her to her assailant on a silver platter.

The lump of guilt that lodged in his throat made it hard for him to swallow. "Are there—" He coughed and tried again. "Are there any suspects?"

"No." Roger shook his head. The man seemed to have aged in the past five minutes, giving Micah a firsthand glimpse into the hell the past couple of months had been for his entire family.

A hell *he* had created.

His chest nearly caved in from the crushing guilt pushing down on it.

"The investigation is still ongoing, of course. In fact, I just spoke to the detective in charge."

"What did he say?" Lila asked.

"That there still is no solid lead," Roger said with a weary sigh, turning his attention back to Micah, "which is why we cannot reveal anything to the press. I hate that Bailey's name is being dragged through the mud, but they are trying to flush out the assailant, and at the moment, finding whoever did this is more important than her reputation."

"Of course," Micah managed to get out.

"It's also the reason for the bodyguards who have been accompanying Bailey everywhere," Lila stated.

"But they will no longer be accompanying me," Bailey interjected.

Roger's forehead creased with annoyance, and Micah could tell that the extra muscle was a point of contention. He was with her father on this one. Now that he knew the entire story, he wouldn't blame the man if he locked her away somewhere.

A thought occurred to him.

"That's why you were gone these past few weeks," Micah said, the picture becoming clearer.

Roger nodded. "We thought it was safer to have Bailey out of the country."

Micah turned to Bailey. "If the kidnapper hasn't been caught, why did you come back?"

Her father grunted, his lips thinned with irritation.

"I refuse to hide anymore," Bailey said with a defiant lift of her chin. "I didn't leave one prison only to come back to New York and get locked in another one. That's another reason I want to do this documentary—to show the person who kidnapped me that he did not break me."

"He could have *killed* you," her father stated.

"But he didn't," she countered. She turned to Micah. "I want to show all those people who doubted me that Bailey Hamilton is back and better than ever."

"Do we have your word you'll keep this information that we've shared private?" Roger Hamilton asked.

"Absolutely," Micah said. "I truly am sorry for any

role my show played in this. The last thing I want to do is cause any more harm."

"No one blames you," Lila said.

They didn't have to blame him. Micah blamed himself.

He turned to Bailey. "I don't want anything else to happen to you."

"Let's make sure that nothing does," Roger said.

As they made their way down the hall to Daniel's office, Bailey realized Micah had been eerily quiet in the ten minutes since the meeting with her mother and father had ended. She was still shocked at how quickly her parents had capitulated, and now that they were both on board, she was ready to move forward. The quicker they got started, the quicker she could get on the road to normalcy.

Insisting that Daniel be part of the production team had popped into her head out of nowhere, but Bailey was grateful for the idea. Her brother had gone overboard in his overprotectiveness lately, but he would be an ally. Daniel wouldn't let anyone take advantage of her.

Although part of her wouldn't mind if Micah decided to take advantage of her, just a little bit. Heat flushed Bailey's skin at the deliciously wicked thought. She looked over at him and noticed the worry lines creasing his forehead.

"Are you okay?" she asked.

Micah glanced over at her, and the look in his eyes told the story of the turmoil undoubtedly taking place inside him.

"I'm so sorry, Bailey. I had no idea what really happened to you."

"That's a good thing," she said. "It means we're doing a good job of keeping it out of the news. According to the police, it's imperative that the abduction is kept under wraps while they investigate."

"It sounds as if the investigation is going slowly," he said.

"As far as I know, they've questioned just about everyone I was in contact with that week, along with several models and a couple of my old boyfriends." She shrugged. "But so far, nothing."

"This is my fault," he said. Bailey was so shocked that she stopped walking.

"Why would you say that?" she asked.

"Because it is," Micah said in a strained voice. He shut his eyes and pitched his head back. The pain on his face caused her heart to pinch. When he looked back at her, his eyes were filled with remorse. "I'm the one who pressured you into revealing your preshow ritual. It's my fault that whoever kidnapped you knew you were going to be there alone."

"That's completely ridiculous," Bailey said. If anyone was to blame it was her. She should have known better than to put so much information about herself out there. "Micah, this was not your fault," Bailey reiterated, but he was having none of that.

He looked to be in absolute agony.

Bailey put her hand on his forearm and gave him a gentle squeeze. "Micah, listen to me. This was *not* your fault."

Micah looked down at her hand, then back to her face, his eyes boring into hers. The power of their connection was unmistakable, its affects unavoidable. Her skin tingled where she touched him, and it took more effort than usual to push breath out of her lungs.

Bailey removed her hand and took a step back. She cleared her throat and said, "My routine isn't some highly guarded secret. My attacker could have found out about it from a number of different sources. Please, don't blame yourself for this. The man who kidnapped me is to blame here, no one else."

The irony of her words smacked Bailey in the face. She had been blaming herself for weeks, trying to figure out what she could have done to prevent her kidnapping. Could she have been more vigilant? Could she have fought off the attacker if she had been paying closer attention to her surroundings? The second-guessing had become a constant part of her life.

"Hopefully, eventually, the person who did this will be brought to justice," she continued. "For now, I just want to get on with my life. And this documentary will be a huge step forward for me. I want to talk to Daniel right now so we can get started as soon as possible."

Bailey still wasn't sure he was convinced, but he nodded.

She forced a smile as she gestured for him to follow her to Daniel's office. She found her brother behind his desk, hunched over his computer screen.

Bailey rapped on his slightly ajar door. "Hey, are you busy?"

Daniel's head popped up and his eyes instantly zeroed in on Micah.

"Give me a minute," he said. He took a few moments to finish up whatever he was doing behind his massive computer screen before coming around his desk.

"Daniel, this is Micah Jones. Micah, my brother Daniel Hamilton."

"Your reputation precedes you," Micah said, extending his right hand.

"Likewise," Daniel replied, accepting the handshake. The tension radiating between the two of them was palpable. Bailey barely resisted rolling her eyes.

Men.

Daniel turned to her and gestured to Micah. "What's going on here? I know you're not going back on his show after the press conference debacle."

"It was not a debacle," she argued, even though she knew full well it had been. "And I'm not doing an interview. I've agreed to participate in a documentary that Micah wants to premier on his show."

Daniel's forehead immediately dipped into a frown. "A documentary? Whose idea was this?" he asked, his voice drenched in suspicion. He eyed Micah as if he were a snake ready to attack.

Just as she'd anticipated, Bailey had to rehash the same pitch she and Micah had just presented to her parents, fighting off interruptions from Daniel after every other sentence.

"Mom and Dad are both on board with this," she told him. "They both see that this will be a good thing, not only for RHD, but for me, as well. Fashion Week was supposed to be my big moment, Daniel, but I never got the chance. This documentary can give me my second chance."

"You're on the verge of becoming one of the most famous models in the world, Bailey. You don't need some documentary."

Bailey's shoulders wilted in exasperation. She was not up for fighting Daniel on this.

"Your sister's name is being dragged through the mud," Micah said. "I want to give Bailey the opportunity to tell her side of the story."

"Exactly. This is a good thing, Daniel, but I told Micah that I wouldn't do it if you weren't part of it."

Bailey could tell that he was not happy about that, and it made her even more grateful that she'd gotten her parents' blessing first. Their approval knocked the wind out of the sails of any protest Daniel could muster.

"Please," she told her brother. "I need to do this, Daniel."

"There's only one thing you need to do right now—stay safe," her brother said. His eyes widened as he looked at Micah, and Bailey realized that he thought he'd just let the cat out of the bag.

"It's okay," Bailey said. "Micah knows about the abduction. Dad told him. He figured if we're going to do this, then Micah needed to know the full story."

"How do you know you can trust him?"

"Why wouldn't she?" Micah asked.

"We still don't know who attacked Bailey. And you *were* the last person to interview her. I wouldn't put it past a reporter to stage this whole thing, then come around offering to do an exclusive story on her," Daniel said, taking a menacing step forward.

Micah simply crossed his arms over his chest and maintained his cool and calm stance, which Bailey knew would only piss Daniel off even more. Her brother took another step forward, bringing himself and Micah practically nose to nose. Bailey stepped between the two men and spread her arms wide.

"Seriously?" She turned to her brother. "Enough with the conspiracy theories, Daniel. Micah did not have me kidnapped. Think of how ridiculous that sounds." She looked at her brother, pleading with him to look past his misgivings and focus on the bigger picture. "I want to do this. And I want you to be part of it. Please, say you'll do it."

Although his eyes still shot daggers at Micah, Daniel reluctantly capitulated.

"Fine," he said. When he looked at her, the concern filling his eyes was so deep it tugged at Bailey's soul. "I just want to make sure no one takes advantage of you."

"That's a good thing, because I don't want to be taken advantage of. That's the reason I want you on this project."

"No one is going to take advantage of you," Micah assured her.

"You're damn right about that," Daniel spat.

"I also want you in on this because I trust your insight and I know you'll make sure the documentary is amazing," Bailey said, trying to defuse the tension.

"I can keep you safe *and* make sure the documentary is good," Daniel said.

"So can I," Micah argued.

Bailey shut her eyes and brought both hands up to rub her temples.

What had she gotten herself into?

Chapter 5

It had only been an hour, but Bailey was already over the camera following her around. She was okay with the occasional interview, or being videoed when she was on the runway or during a photo shoot, but having a camera practically capturing her every move was a pain in the butt. Why on earth would reality-TV stars subject themselves to this?

She pretended to pay attention to what Louisa Martinez, one of the junior designers of RHD's resort-wear collection, was telling her, but Bailey's focus was on Micah, who was standing just a few feet away, his eyes following her. It made her uncomfortable in an entirely different way. No, not uncomfortable, just… overly aware. Arousal prickled along her nerve endings at his nearness.

"The sarong should drape effortlessly," Louisa said.

She took a length of sage-and-yellow-striped fabric and wrapped it around Bailey's waist.

Bailey raised her arms and peered down at the material, gently twisting her hips. "Seems pretty effortless to me."

"Do you like the pattern?"

"I think this one is a lot better than the bright orange and yellow," Bailey said. "It's more subtle, and it complements the other pieces in the collection."

She may not have been a designer, but she had grown up in this place. She had an eye for fashion and was used to the junior designers seeking her opinion. Bailey didn't mind, especially if it was for someone who had potential, like Louisa. The fashion industry was as cutthroat for designers as it was for models. She wanted the RHD team members who really put in the effort to succeed.

"Bailey." She looked up to find Brianna waving her over. "We're ready for you."

Louisa unwrapped the fabric from her waist and Bailey started for the open space toward the back of the second floor, where a mock beach scene had been set up. They were doing a preliminary photo shoot featuring RHD's new resort-wear line. The real shoot would take place on St. Barts, but Daniel wanted to get some initial shots so that he and his team could get a feel for the advertising campaign.

Two reflective photography umbrellas and a lighting rig had been set up. A flowing silky blue fabric covered the rear wall. Sand had been brought in and liberally spread across the floor. Palm trees that looked remarkably real completed the set.

"We'll start with the swimwear first," Brianna said, handing Bailey a two-piece.

As she took the wisp of fabric from her sister's hands, Bailey inadvertently felt her face heat with embarrassment.

She was appalled at her reaction.

She was a professional, damn it! She'd been modeling swimwear for a decade. What was the deal with this sudden awkwardness?

Maybe it was because she could practically feel Micah's eyes following her as she headed for the changing room at the end of the hallway. She glanced back to find him staring. His face was a blank mask, but the heat in his eyes scorched her.

Bailey shut the door behind her and leaned against it, covering her chest with her hand.

"Good God," she whispered.

Okay, so the camera constantly shadowing her wasn't the only thing she had to worry about when it came to this documentary. She had to figure out a better way to deal with the hours she was destined to spend in close proximity to Micah.

And to think she'd purposely signed herself up for this. She must be losing her mind.

Bailey took a moment to remind herself of what was at stake. So what if she had to endure bouts of mind-altering lust under Micah's heated gaze? The important thing was that the world would see that she was the same Bailey Hamilton she had always been. Even more important, her kidnapper would see it, too.

Besides, she had ways of dealing with lust when she

was alone at night. It had been so long since she'd been in a relationship that she had pretty much mastered every self-pleasuring technique out there.

This is so not the time to think about that.

She was finally back to work. She needed to focus.

She donned the bikini. It was one of Kyle's designs—bold fuchsia tropical flowers on a black background. She slipped into the wedge sandals Brianna had also given her, and wrapped a solid fuchsia sarong around her waist.

The tidal wave of self-consciousness that pummeled her when she stepped out of the changing room was unappreciated, but completely understandable, and even a bit expected.

And it wasn't just because of Micah and those hot glances he'd been sending her way all morning.

This was the first time she'd worked in any capacity as a model since that fateful night back in September. For weeks Bailey had been telling herself that it would be easy to jump in right where she'd left off. This was, after all, what she did for a living.

But deep down, Bailey had known the truth. The kidnapping had forever changed her. She would have to learn how to adjust to modeling in the AAE—the After-Abduction Era.

And even though appearing in a bathing suit before Micah's ever-watchful eyes wasn't the only thing contributing to her self-consciousness, it was definitely a big factor. Pictures of her clad in similar—sometimes even tinier—bikinis had appeared in magazines, on billboards and all over the internet. Yet the thought of walking onto the beach set while he looked on had her skin pebbling with goose bumps *and* flushing with heat.

It would have helped if Micah was just a bit more adept in hiding what he was thinking when he stared at her. The look in his eyes was so inappropriate that he could not have been conscious of what he was doing, especially with a half dozen people surrounding them. His gaze trailed her from the moment she returned to the set, traveling the length of her body in a slow perusal.

Bailey resigned herself to the fact that her nipples would give her away. There was no chance of hiding her reaction in what she was wearing.

"Are we going to do this or what?" Daniel practically growled. He was looking at Micah with daggers in his eyes, which told her that her brother hadn't missed the way Micah had been staring at her.

Micah coughed and averted his eyes. He walked over to his cameraman and began to consult with him.

Daniel still looked ready to commit murder as he adjusted the seaweed that had been made to look as if it had washed ashore. Brianna stood to the side, smirking. The makeup artist was completely oblivious to the tension in the room as she touched up Bailey's cheeks.

Bailey forced Micah, her siblings, her nerves and everything else out of her mind as she took her spot next to the fake palm tree. As soon as their in-house photographer, Julian, raised his camera, everything else ceased to exist.

An overwhelming sense of rightness washed over her. This was what she lived for; it was what had been missing these past two months. She was back in her element, back to doing the thing she loved the most.

And it felt amazing.

Micah stood in absolute awe as he watched Bailey come alive in front of the camera. He knew he should stop staring, or at the very least figure out a way to close his mouth. But he couldn't tear his eyes away from her if his life depended on it.

From the moment Bailey appeared dressed in that wisp of a bathing suit, every single fiber of his being had been enraptured by her.

But it wasn't just the way her incredible body filled out the bathing suit. It was the transformation that had taken place before his very eyes that had him completely and utterly amazed.

There was something about Bailey's behavior that had been eating away at Micah since their meeting at the coffee shop a couple of days ago. There was this frailty about her, a vulnerability that was so unlike the vibrant woman who constantly turned heads wherever she went. For the first time since before her disappearance, Micah saw *that* Bailey again. The minute the photographer began to shoot, the shy, timid Bailey ceased to exist.

It was hard to tear his eyes away from her.

When he did, he found Daniel Hamilton staring at him yet again, his expression murderous.

This was going to be a problem. Why Bailey insisted her brother be part of the production team was beyond him. It was only the first day of filming and they were already butting heads. It probably didn't help that Daniel had caught Micah staring at his sister as if he wanted to eat her for breakfast, lunch and dinner.

Which he did. For at least a solid week.

Micah bit back a groan. He couldn't look at her in that skimpy bikini a second longer without showing the entire crew just how much he was dying to have a taste of Bailey.

He turned away from the scene to consult with his cameraman, Ben, about which shots he wanted, and Ben began circling the perimeter of the room, taking in the entire scene.

The rapid clicks of the photographer's shutter opening and closing provided the soundtrack, along with his commands for Bailey to tilt her chin up, lower her shoulder, soften her eyes. One of the assistant designers held a portable fan about three feet away from her, the breeze causing Bailey's luxurious dark and light brown locks to delicately whirl around her face.

God, she was gorgeous.

Micah's mouth watered at the sight of her firm, trim thigh peeking through the slit in the sarong as she posed. The look was casual, her smile sweet but slightly seductive. And unbelievably sexy.

Micah's gut tightened. How in the hell was he supposed to make it through these next few weeks? If the lust didn't kill him, Daniel Hamilton probably would.

After several more shots, the photographer rose from the crouched position he'd held for the past twenty minutes and said, "I think we've got enough to start with."

As quickly as Bailey's shield had come down once the camera had started snapping, it went right back up again. The bold, self-assured woman who'd commanded the attention of everyone in the room was gone, only to be replaced by this reserved shell of her former self.

It was as if she had a split personality.

Micah looked around to see if anyone had noticed, but they were all just going about their day as if she hadn't transformed right before their eyes.

"That was good," Brianna told her sister. "You haven't lost a step."

"Thanks," Bailey said with a relieved smile. "It felt great to be in front of the camera again."

"Were you afraid it wouldn't feel the same?" Micah asked without thinking.

Brianna and Bailey both turned to him.

"What?" Bailey asked.

Micah cleared his throat. It was obvious to him what was going on here, but he wasn't sure if Bailey was ready to face it, or if she even fully grasped it.

"This was the first time that you've modeled in the past two months, wasn't it? Were you afraid that it wouldn't feel the same?"

She threaded her arms through the robe the assistant designer handed her and belted it at the waist. Then she looked up at him again and said, "Yes. I'm almost ashamed to admit it, but I was terrified that I would step in front of the camera and freeze."

To hear her admit her fear in that soft, vulnerable voice set off a dull ache within his chest. He knew how much modeling meant to her. It was her life. That she had feared for even a second that she wouldn't be able to do the thing that was so dear to her made Micah want to kill the person who had abducted her with his bare hands.

"I was worried that it would take me a while to find my mojo, but it didn't." A proud grin spread across Bailey's face. "I felt right at home."

"It showed," Micah said. "You looked amazing."

Brianna cleared her throat, and Micah snapped to attention. For a second there he'd forgotten that he and Bailey were surrounded by a half dozen people, and a camera that was catching every move they made.

Damn. He had to get it together. He had a job to do, an executive producer position to win. He couldn't let this mind-numbing attraction to Bailey distract him from his goal.

Although ever since he'd learned the truth behind Bailey's disappearance, the driving force behind this project had morphed into something else. His eyes were still on the EP position, but winning it had taken a backseat to something more important.

He owed it to Bailey to make this documentary the best it could be.

She might not blame him for what happened to her, but Micah had no doubt that her interview on *Connect* had played a role. If he hadn't asked her to reveal her prerunway ritual, her kidnapper wouldn't have known about the alone time she indulged in before a show. She would never have been assaulted, wouldn't have had those drugs planted on her. The ugly rumors about her being a cocaine addict wouldn't be plastered across the headlines.

He was the one who had caused this mess in her life.

And why?

Because he'd wanted—no, he'd *needed*—to know as much about her as she was willing to share. It was because of this insane attraction to her that he'd pressed so hard during their interview. Back in September, as she'd sat across from him on the set of *Connect,* Micah had been enchanted by her. He'd gone off script, asking questions that had not been preplanned, pressing her for details about her life. It had made for good television. How could he have known that he'd inadvertently driven her right into the clutches of a kidnapper who could have easily taken her life?

The fear of what could have happened to her stole his breath, and guilt over the part he'd played in it ate a hole in his gut.

His insatiable need to learn all he could about Bailey had created this mess, and it was his job to clean it up. As difficult as that was sure to be, he would have to figure out a way to put a lid on his feelings for Bailey. His attraction to her could have cost her her life. He wouldn't allow it to cloud his judgment again.

Chapter 6

Micah couldn't help but be mesmerized as he sat across from Lila Hamilton. It was more than obvious where the Hamilton daughters had acquired their beauty and their sense of style and grace. The woman still had it. To say she had aged gracefully was an understatement. Lila Hamilton would be considered a knockout by anyone's standards.

And she was fiercely protective of her youngest daughter.

"If you had to describe Bailey in one word, what would it be?" Micah asked.

"Loyal," she answered without hesitation.

"Loyalty seems to be a central characteristic of every member of the Hamilton family."

"We appreciate what we have, and we understand

that we must stick together in order to keep our family's vision alive."

Micah nodded. His admiration for the way the family operated grew every day he was around them. He and Ben had been coming to the studio for a week, and not once had Micah encountered anything more substantial than a quiet disagreement between the siblings. If anyone were to look for drama when they watched the documentary, they would be in for major disappointment.

A nerve in Micah's jaw twitched as he recalled a discussion he'd had with Rebecca Barrington, one of the producers at WLNY, before he'd come to RHD this morning. Rebecca had stressed the importance of getting the dirt on Bailey. She was looking for exactly what Micah had promised Roger Hamilton he *wouldn't* deliver—some sleazy drama-filled exposé.

Micah refused to go that route. He wouldn't break his promise to Bailey by creating drama where there was none, simply for the sake of ratings.

"Just a couple more questions," he said, returning to his one-on-one with Lila Hamilton. "A couple of your older children followed in your husband's footsteps and became designers, but Bailey decided to try *your* first love, modeling. Were you surprised?"

A gorgeous smile drew across Lila's face as she laughed. "Not at all. Both Bailey and Brianna loved playing dress-up as children, but where Brianna was all about making sure that the outfits were coordinated, Bailey just wanted to strut across the living room. She didn't care what she looked like, as long as all eyes were on her."

Micah could just imagine a five-year-old Bailey draped in her mother's oversize clothes, trying to walk in shoes that were too big for her.

"Having been a model yourself before you became a designer, were you ever afraid of the type of things Bailey might encounter in the modeling world?"

Lila folded her hands in her lap. "I've always been a bit overprotective of Bailey, probably because she will always be my baby. When she told me she wanted to become a model, I tried to prepare her for the darker side of the industry. She's worked mainly for RHD, so she has been somewhat sheltered, but unfortunately, she has had a taste of the more sinister aspects of the profession. There are only a few top spots in the fashion world at a given time, and Bailey has had to deal with her share of jealousy."

"It must be hard as a mother to see your child suffer."

"It is." Lila raised her shoulder in a hapless shrug. "I can protect her for only so long. After a certain point, I have to let her live. Bailey is a lot stronger than many people give her credit for."

Over this past week, Micah had witnessed Bailey's strength on several occasions. Although she was still reserved, she didn't hesitate to make her opinions known. She'd stood up to Daniel a few times when he'd tried to change aspects of the shoot.

She'd also stood up to *him*. It had turned him on way more than it should have, to the point where Micah had begun to suggest things that he knew she would disapprove of, just so he could see that fire in her eyes.

Once Lila's interview was done, he gathered RHD's in-house photographer, Julian; one of the younger up-and-coming designers whose work had been featured in the Fashion Week show; and Suzanne, a makeup artist. All three worked closely with Bailey on a regular basis. Micah tried not to be jealous, but damn, how could he not be? He was jealous of anyone who didn't have to make up excuses to be around her.

He wondered if these three knew just how lucky they were.

The retro '70s-style chair that Lila Hamilton had sat in for her interview had been replaced by three stools, set up against the nondescript bluish-gray backdrop. Micah perched on the stool facing them and began.

"What is it like working with Bailey Hamilton?" He posed the question to the entire panel.

"It's horrible," Julian said.

"She's a slave driver," Suzanne put in.

"And a diva," said the designer.

Micah was stunned speechless, until all three laughed to the point that they nearly fell off the stools.

"Now that the comedy hour is over," Julian said, "we'll tell you about the real Bailey."

And, just as he'd expected, the praise the three heaped on Bailey made her seem almost too good to be true.

"I've worked with more models in the industry than I can count, but none are as low-key and low-maintenance as Bailey," Suzanne said. "I remember years ago, during her very first Fashion Week, there was some mix-up with the dressing room, and we couldn't get in to do her makeup until twenty minutes before she was scheduled to hit the runway. I was running around like a madwoman, but Bailey was as cool and calm as can be. You would have thought she was the seasoned veteran and I was the newcomer."

"She just has this vibe about her, as if nothing can go wrong, and even if something does, she'll just work through it," Julian said. "Compared to the divas in this business who are ready to fall away in a dead faint if a single hair is out of place, Bailey is a breath of fresh air."

As Micah listened to them heap praise upon her, the yearning he'd developed for Bailey blossomed into an all-consuming need. He'd known she was special. And, apparently, everyone else knew it, too.

He had counted on today being a reprieve from the nearly debilitating desire that seized his brain whenever he was around her, but the interviews with Bailey's family and coworkers only made Micah want her more. Despite his best efforts, Micah found himself falling—hard. He knew he should fight it, but damn, it would be easier to wash the windows of every skyscraper in Manhattan.

Today, he'd learned that Bailey was so much more than the pretty face and incredible body that had filled his dreams with mind-bending fantasies for the past week. She was genuine, giving and fiercely loyal. She was the kind of woman a man would give anything and everything just to be near.

She was the kind of woman worth falling in love with…and Micah found himself doing just that.

Bailey accepted the insulated cup from Zoe as she came around the table.

"The coffee shop was out of raw sugar, so I used honey instead."

Bailey took a sip of the lavender-scented tea. "This is perfect," she assured her.

Zoe had just begun her new career as host of an hour-long show called *Fashion Express,* but when she wasn't filming, she could be found at RHD. Usually huddled up in Kyle's office.

Bailey nodded toward Kyle's computer screen. "What do you think of outer space as a theme for the fashion show?"

Zoe's scrunched-up face told Bailey exactly what she thought of the idea.

"Fine, so outer space is out of the question." She laughed. She'd been racking her brain, trying to come up with a fresh, authentic theme for the upcoming show.

"Exactly what's wrong with the beach theme again?" Zoe asked. "The show is for the resort-wear collection."

"It's just so predictable," Bailey said. "All eyes are going to be on RHD. We need to come up with something that will have people talking until the next Fashion Week and beyond."

Benjamin sneezed and both Bailey and Zoe looked up.

"Sorry," he said.

"Bless you," Bailey replied with a smile. For a moment, she had forgotten that he was even there. She'd become surprisingly used to Ben following her around. She was still overly cognizant of what she said and did, but she was no longer hyperaware of the camera tracking every step she took.

She was aware, however, of Micah Jones's larger-than-life presence. He was everywhere, like a constant feeling on her skin. Even when he wasn't physically present—like now, when he was conducting interviews on the fourth floor—just knowing he was in the building was enough to make her stomach flutter and her breath hitch.

But he'd stayed stubbornly true to his earlier assertion that their relationship should remain strictly professional. Other than those instances when she'd caught him watching her with that intense, raw desire in his eyes, Micah had maintained his distance.

It was for the best. She knew this. But knowing that it was wise not to fall for him and actually stopping herself from doing so were two entirely different things.

How could she *not* fall for him? Not taking into account the obvious—that he was smart, handsome and had enough sexy swagger to make her mouth water—he was also the most thoughtful man she'd encountered outside of her father and brothers.

It was the little things, like bringing her crumpets from an uptown bakery she'd mentioned the other day, and, now that she thought about it, the big things, too, like actually listening to her ideas about the documentary. Those were the things that had thoughts of Micah—

some of them highly inappropriate—wandering around her brain much too often lately.

"I still think the beach theme is the best option," Zoe said, knocking her out of her lustful musings.

"I don't know," Bailey hedged.

"Something nautical. Think soft blues and white, something that reflects cool and comfort."

"Ice!" Bailey exclaimed.

"What?"

"How about a winter theme?"

"For resort wear?"

"Why not?" Bailey asked, excitement building as she pictured the scene. "It's the perfect contrast, and it would be totally unexpected. Think about it. We'll have snow-covered boulders, icicles, maybe a few barren trees. Then we bring out RHD's resort wear, perfect for shaking off the cold of winter."

Zoe tilted her head to the side and tapped her polished nails against the desk. "You know, that may not be such a bad idea."

"It's a great idea," Bailey said. She nudged Zoe's arm. "Admit it, you like it."

Zoe rolled her eyes, but a playful smile inched up one side of her mouth. "Okay, I admit that you just hit it out of the park. A winter theme is fabulous."

Bailey laughed at the reluctance she heard in Zoe's voice. She was so happy that Kyle had come to his senses and admitted his feelings for Zoe. Her future sister-in-law fit in perfectly with their family.

The sound of footsteps approaching drew Bailey's

attention, but it was hearing her name that made her stand up straight.

"We have to make sure Bailey doesn't see this," Kyle said as he entered his office, looking down at something he held in his hands. He was followed by Brianna, who stopped dead in her tracks when she spotted Bailey.

"You have to make sure I don't see what?" Bailey demanded.

"Shit," Kyle said, folding a tabloid and sticking it under his arm.

Bailey held out her palm. "Hand it over."

"It'll just upset you," Brianna said.

Bailey remained where she stood, palm out.

With a groan, Kyle slapped the paper into her hand. Bailey read the headline, and her blood instantly started to boil.

Bailey Hamilton Suffering from an Exotic Medical Condition.

Underneath the headline was a photo of her entering a medical building on the Upper West Side.

"Are you kidding me?" Bailey screeched. "I was going to the dentist for a cleaning!"

She skimmed the article, which postulated that the reason behind her disappearance and continued seclusion was that she had been diagnosed with a rare disease and was being treated with medication and intensive therapy.

She slammed the paper down on Kyle's desk. "I'm in seclusion because I can't step outside without the press hounding me with questions and twisting around my answers whenever I do answer them."

Just then, Micah walked into the office, followed by the second cameraman who'd been brought in for the special interviews with RHD employees.

Bailey put both hands up. "No taping," she ordered. "I'm on the verge of a nervous breakdown and I'd rather not have it captured for posterity."

Micah's forehead creased in a frown. "What's going on?" he asked.

Kyle picked up the tabloid and tossed it to him.

Bailey paced back and forth in front of her brother's desk, trying to calm herself down. It wasn't working.

Would her life ever be her own again?

The unfairness of this entire situation made her want to rage against the world. She had not done anything wrong. In fact, she'd done everything she could to live her life completely aboveboard. She'd been warned countless times about the dangers of the industry. She'd witnessed firsthand how quickly one could fall from grace, and she'd steered clear of those pitfalls.

Bailey wanted to show that all models were not anorexic druggies who partied all night. Sure, she'd attended a fair number of industry bashes, and she'd been known to hit a club or two, but she also volunteered at the Boys & Girls Club of New York and sponsored a week-long character-building workshop for inner-city girls every year.

Whenever she did an interview, she made sure she showcased all the positive things that had happened in her life because of modeling. Yet the same media that once praised her for always keeping her nose clean were now doing everything they could to eviscerate her good name.

"It should be clear to anyone who bothers to look hard enough that I am just fine. What am I supposed to do—stand in the middle of Times Square and shout it at the top of my lungs?"

"Oh, yeah, that will convince people that you're not crazy," Kyle snorted.

Bailey glared at her brother.

"You don't have to do anything," Brianna said. "Let the press say what they want. Who cares?"

"*I* care," Bailey said. "And so should you and everyone else here at RHD. The longer they speculate about what's going on with me, the more it affects the brand. I'm just ready for this to end."

"Bailey, Roger Hamilton Designs can handle whatever hits it takes. The important thing is keeping you safe," Brianna insisted.

"Stop downplaying what this is costing RHD," Bailey said. "Image is everything in this business, and rumors of me on drugs, or hiding some secret medical condition, or whatever else is being said is not good for RHD's image."

Of everything that had happened following her abduction, it was the backlash RHD had taken that caused Bailey the most pain. She hated to think that the company her parents had built together would suffer because of her.

"I need to convince the media that I'm not this person they're making me out to be."

"Don't tell them," Micah said. "Show them."

Every eye in the room turned to him.

"*Telling* the media that you're fine isn't going to get you anywhere," Micah continued. "Before September, you were a regular on Page Six, but now you go from your apartment to this studio. If you want to show reporters that you really are back and better than ever, you need to get out there and actually show them, actually *be* the Bailey you were before your attack."

"I have to agree with Micah on this one," Kyle remarked in a tone that said agreeing with Micah was akin to eating dirt. Her brothers were obviously still leery of him.

"So what do you suggest? Should I call up the press corps and tell them to head to Fifth Avenue so they can get some shots of me buying socks at Bloomingdale's?"

"You won't have to call anyone," Micah said. "All you have to do is step outside and you'll have more than enough press following your every move. But I was thinking more along the lines of a nightclub than a shopping trip to Bloomingdale's."

Bailey groaned. "The last thing I'm in the mood for is a night of clubbing. Having to fight off the media is one thing, but dealing with jerks with weak pickup lines is more than I can handle right now."

"You wouldn't have to worry about guys trying to pick you up," Micah said.

"Yeah," Kyle started, "the bodyguards can—"

"No," Bailey said with an emphatic shake of her head. "I finally convinced Mom and Dad to get rid of the bodyguards just yesterday. I'm not going back to being escorted around."

"You wouldn't have to worry about hiring bodyguards," Micah said.

She folded her arms across her chest. "Are you planning to run interference?"

"Yes."

Such a simple word, but it was spoken with such potency, such resoluteness, that Bailey immediately felt safer. She had no doubts that Micah was ready, willing and more than able to play the role of personal bodyguard if that was what she required.

Maybe this wasn't a bad idea. The press would have no reason to dig if she was out there for everyone to see. If there was even the slightest chance that it would help to put some of the rumors to rest…

"It's up to you, Bailey. Just remember that the longer you shy away from the press, the longer you'll see these types of headlines. You need to get back out there and remind people who you are."

"Micah's right," Brianna said. "But I'm not sure if the club scene is the best environment for you right now. Maybe something a bit more subdued and less crowded would be better."

"I can make that happen," Micah said. "A friend of mine just opened a new place in the Meatpacking District. It's small, intimate and a lot tamer than the flashier clubs in Midtown. It would be a more controlled environment."

The more Bailey thought about it, the more she warmed up to the idea of a night out. She needed to be seen doing the things she used to do, being the girl she used to be. She hadn't felt like that girl in months; she needed to rediscover the old Bailey.

But what if she couldn't?

The idea that she would never feel like her old self again, that the kidnapping had irrevocably changed her, sent a now-familiar whisper of dread along her skin.

Bailey turned to Micah. "I'm in," she said.

"Bailey—" Brianna started, but Bailey cut her off.

"I want to go to your friend's club. How does Friday night sound to you?"

Micah blinked several times before saying, "Friday night is fine with me."

"Good," Bailey said with a firm nod. "It's a date."

Chapter 7

Micah let out a low whistle as he walked up to the imposing building on Central Park West. He had to make a conscious effort to stop his jaw from dropping open when he stepped into the luxurious lobby, with its glittering chandeliers and gleaming marble columns. This was definitely how the other half lived.

Trying not to seem like some bum off the street who had never seen nice things before, Micah resisted stopping in the middle of the lobby to stare at his surroundings. Instead, he strode with purpose toward the doorman behind the reception desk.

After being confirmed on the list of visitors, Micah was shown to the elevators. He watched the numbers climb as he ascended to the tenth floor.

With each floor he passed, his skin grew hotter until he was ready to strip off his brushed-suede jacket. Up to this point, he'd done a credible job of lying to himself. He'd insisted that he was doing this for Bailey's sake. He'd offered to accompany her for a night on the town not just to get the press off her back, but because he saw that she needed to get out and enjoy herself.

It had nothing to do with him damn near dying to be with her every second of every day.

The elevator dinged with his arrival on the tenth floor, and Micah followed the doorman's instructions to Bailey's apartment. He rang the bell and collected his breath. It rushed out of him the second the door opened.

Micah felt as if he'd been punched in the gut at the sight of Bailey. She wore supertight dark blue designer jeans with a bright yellow sequined top. Her black leather jacket ended just above her waist and hugged her curves. Her sky-high heels had to be at least five inches. They were snakeskin, in the same yellow as her top. She looked amazing. Stunning. Irresistible.

Her thick flowing hair was slicked to the side, with a yellow flower holding it in place. It tumbled down her back, tempting him to run his fingers through it, to feel its softness. Micah clutched his fists to stop himself from satisfying his curiosity.

She was a chameleon—a demure, hauntingly beautiful creature one minute and a fierce fashion model the next.

"Hello," she said, taking a step back. "Come in. I'm almost ready."

"Thanks," Micah said. He entered the apartment and allowed his eyes to wander. It was as lavish as the rest of the building, but the decor was much more modern, better suited to the two young women who lived here.

"You look really nice," he said.

Biggest understatement in the history of the universe.

"Thank you," Bailey said. "You look great yourself." She smiled, and his blood began to burn with that all-consuming desire that simmered just underneath the surface.

Micah knew better than to reveal how much of a sucker punch her appearance had given him. Despite what tonight might look like to the casual observer, Bailey was still his subject. Journalistic integrity had to be upheld if anyone was to take this documentary seriously. It would be hard as hell to claim impartiality if he got caught with his tongue hanging out of his mouth like a salivating cartoon character.

"Can you give me just a few more minutes to finish getting ready? I promise I won't be long. Have a seat," she said, motioning to the sofa. "Can I get you something to drink?"

"I'm good," Micah said as he sat. He popped up seconds later as Brianna entered the room.

"Hi, Brianna."

"Hello," she said. "So you and Bailey are going to a club after all?"

"Yes," he said. "It's my friend's newest. I think Bailey will like it. It's a slightly older crowd, not the college scene, you know?"

"That's good." Brianna nodded. "She needs to ease her way back into the social scene. It sounds like the kind of place that won't be too overwhelming." She looked over her shoulder, back toward the hallway where Bailey had retreated, then took a few steps toward him. In a much lower voice, she said, "Be careful with her, Micah."

He understood where Brianna was coming from, but Micah was starting to understand Bailey's side of this, too. Her family was shielding her not just from her attacker, but from the world. The more they kept her hidden, the more speculation she would draw.

"I won't let anything happen to your sister," Micah said.

Brianna came even closer. "Look, we haven't told Bailey any of this, but there have been several other occurrences that lead us to believe that Bailey's kidnapping was not an isolated incident."

Trepidation clawed up Micah's spine. "What are you talking about, Brianna?"

"Just…things," she said. "Kyle's tires were slashed, and before that, he and Zoe were both locked in a supply closet at the Childs International Hotel. There have been a couple of things at RHD, too."

"Why haven't you all told Bailey?"

"Because we don't want to alarm her."

Micah had never heard anything more ridiculous in his life. Bailey was in more danger than he first thought, and they were deliberately keeping her in the dark. And, worse, they thought it was for her own good!

"It's more than just the physical threats to her," Brianna continued. "I'm more concerned about this." She tapped the side of her head. "Bailey is still fragile."

"Excuse me, but I am *not* fragile." Micah watched Brianna's eyes slide closed as Bailey stormed into the room.

"What do you think you're doing, Brianna?"

"I was just—"

"Treating me as if I'm some porcelain vase that's about to crack," Bailey said. "I'm stronger than any of you think."

"No one is questioning how strong you are, Bailey."

"Really?" She raised an eyebrow. "Because when I think of fragile, strong isn't the next word that pops into my head. I told you before, I am done being afraid."

Brianna released a tired breath. "Look, I'm sorry, okay? How about if I tag along?"

"You have dinner with Collin," Bailey stated.

"I can cancel."

"Brianna, I can take care of your sister," Micah assured her.

Bailey turned to face him. She put up a finger. "First of all, I don't need you to take care of me. Running interference on sleazebags who try to hit on me? Yes. Playing the big, bad bodyguard? No, thanks. That is not what tonight is about."

Well, it looked as if Feisty Bailey had decided to make an appearance tonight. And in those knockout heels and skintight jeans, she was a thousand times sexier than Micah had ever imagined. He had to will his libido to remain calm.

Brianna put both hands up. "Okay, okay. I just want you to be safe."

"I'll be fine." Bailey enveloped her in a hug. "Now go and get ready for your dinner."

Bailey picked up a wallet no bigger than a deck of cards from the table next to the door and slid the patent-leather strap over her wrist. Micah held the door open for her, then followed her out. He gave Brianna—who looked to be on the verge of snatching Bailey back—a reassuring nod as he closed the door behind them.

Once downstairs, he led Bailey to his car, which he'd parked a half a block away. When they arrived at the club, there was already a line stretching around the block. A deep red velvet rope held back the crowd of eager club-goers.

"Pretty popular place," Bailey observed.

"Half those people won't get in. The club only holds about two hundred."

"But we're on the VIP list, right?" she asked, a hint of teasing in her voice.

Micah looked over at her and grinned. "You put the *V,* the *I* and the *P* in VIP, Miss Hamilton."

"Oh, no. I'm not the one with clout here, Mr. Writer, Producer and Host."

"You forgot Director."

Her head fell back with her laughter, and Micah suddenly realized that laughing was something she didn't do very often. It was a pity. Her laugh was as perfect as the rest of her.

He guided Bailey to the club entrance, where the bouncer let them into a narrow corridor that led straight to an elevator. Even though there was room for at least a dozen people on the old service elevator in the renovated warehouse, Micah and Bailey had the car to themselves. When the elevator doors opened on the second floor, they were greeted by Rafe Edmonds, Micah's old college roommate at Harvard.

Like Micah, Rafe had been a scholarship kid. They'd both done pretty well for themselves since their days on Harvard Yard.

"Welcome, welcome, welcome," Rafe said, clasping Micah's hand and pulling him in for a one-armed hug. Dressed in black jeans and a black T-shirt with a jewel-studded Celtic cross on the front, Rafe was probably the most underdressed man in the club. However, his larger-than-life personality more than made up for his understated attire.

"It is an honor and a pleasure to have you grace my club," Rafe said, capturing Bailey's hand and placing a kiss on it. Micah told himself that the shot of annoyance that had just raced down his spine was due to the fact that Bailey was probably uncomfortable with Rafe's public display, and not because he was jealous.

"When Micah told me he was bringing my favorite crush to the club, I told him he was full of shit."

"Am I your crush?" Bailey asked with a laugh.

"Sweetheart, you're every man's crush."

Micah couldn't stop his eye roll, and he could no longer deny what he was feeling was definitely jealousy.

Maybe introducing Bailey to the world's biggest flirt wasn't the best idea he'd ever had.

"Hey, you guys hungry?" Rafe asked.

"Starving, actually," Bailey replied. "I haven't had anything to eat since lunch, and that was only a granola bar."

"We can do better than that. How about I start you

two off with some drinks?" Rafe asked, motioning for them to follow.

Even though it was early, the crowd was a respectable size. Club goers milled about, drinks in hand, conversations flowing. Micah knew from his previous visits that in a few hours there would be twice as many people and the music would be twice as loud.

The sunken hardwood dance floor was rimmed in deep red fluorescent lights that produced a warm glow. Gold-brushed velvet settees and ottomans lined the interior walls. Each seating area was cordoned off with wine-colored curtains and required a thousand-dollar bar tab just for the privilege of sitting there.

"This place is fantastic," Bailey said, her eyes roaming around the club. Micah noticed several people who seemed to have recognized that one of New York's biggest names in fashion was in the building, but so far the crowd was playing it cool.

"How long have you been open?" she asked Rafe.

"A few months," he answered. He stretched his arms out. "It's the first of my soon-to-be empire."

Micah rolled his eyes again.

As they walked to the bistro, which was located toward the rear of the club, a passing couple bumped into Bailey on their way to the dance floor, causing her to jump.

"You're okay," Micah said, cradling her elbow.

She looked over at him and nodded. He could see the war being waged inside her. She was trying to appear cool, but the fear radiating from her was palpable. Micah wondered if her sister had been right. Was it too soon for her? Had he pushed her into doing something she wasn't ready for?

He leaned over and spoke into her ear. "Bailey, if you're uncomfortable, just let me know. We don't have to stay."

"I'm fine," she said.

It was a lie, but Micah didn't dispute her claim. He simply nodded and took a step closer to her.

Rafe led them to a room that was closed off with frosted-glass doors. There were more gold-velvet sofas, but also several bistro tables.

The moment they sat, a hostess produced menus. But Rafe instructed her to bring out a sample of everything.

"I'm still testing the menu," he said. "You two can be my guinea pigs."

Bailey looked over at Micah and with a sly grin asked, "Is that what the *P* in VIP stands for?"

Missing the joke, Rafe started in on Bailey, bombarding her with questions. Micah had warned him that questions regarding her disappearance were off-limits, but that didn't stop his friend from asking her about everything else.

"What about you two?" Bailey asked. "How did you meet?"

"Freshman year at Harvard," Micah answered.

Bailey's head jerked back in surprise. "Harvard? Really?"

Apparently, she hadn't read up on his background the same way Micah had hers, scouring the internet to learn everything about her.

"Both Micah and I were majoring in government,

but he switched to broadcasting around the same time I switched to marketing," Rafe said. "We did all right for ourselves. From the housing projects to practically running a television studio and owning a place like this."

Bailey looked upon Micah with a sense of wonder, and something else. *Pride.* It caused a rush of warmth to seep into his bones.

The server returned in record time with a platter of signature tapas from the menu. Apparently, there were perks to being with the club owner.

"This all looks amazing," Bailey commented.

"Thanks." Rafe beamed, as if he'd personally prepared the dishes. From what Micah could remember, his old college roommate hadn't been able to boil an egg. "You know—" Rafe pointed at her with a bacon-wrapped shrimp "—it's nice to see a model who doesn't insist on eating rabbit food. You're okay with getting your grub on."

Micah had to agree. Over the past week, he'd discovered several things about Bailey that were atypical of what he'd thought was standard for models. Most notable was her complete lack of diva attitude.

If anyone had the right to be a diva, it was Bailey Hamilton. With a face that could grace every single magazine cover in the world and a body to match, she commanded attention simply by existing. But Micah had yet to meet a woman more down-to-earth.

They dined on an array of dishes that were rotated in and out by two table attendants. After nearly an hour of eating and listening to Rafe share stories of their days on the Yard, Rafe was called away to handle an issue with the DJ.

Micah leaned over and, taking a moment to inhale the scent of Bailey's perfume, spoke into her ear. "You know we can't hide back here all night, right?"

"You sure about that?" she asked with a tense laugh. "This seems like the perfect place to hide."

"You do remember why we're here, don't you, Bailey?"

"Yes." She sighed. "I guess it's time for me to go out and be seen."

Micah captured her wrist. He took her hand between his and rubbed the soft, smooth skin. "You don't have to do this if you're not ready, Bailey."

"I'm ready," she said.

As they left the back room and headed for the dance floor, Micah spotted one of the eager jerks Bailey had warned him about sidling up to her. He caught the discomfort etched across her face and stepped in front of her in a heartbeat.

"Can I help you?" Micah asked the guy.

"Step off, man. I was just asking for a dance."

"Actually, she promised me the next dance." Micah stared down the twentysomething, who looked as if he wasn't old enough to buy a drink. Where in the hell did this youngster get off thinking he could step up to a woman like Bailey?

With his hand on the small of her back, Micah guided her to the middle of the dance floor.

"Thank you," she said. "I'm not in the mood for dealing with that tonight."

"I told you I'd take care of you, didn't I?"

She looked up at him. "Yes," she said. "Thank you."

The up-tempo song ended and a much slower ballad began. Bailey brought her arms up and folded her hands behind Micah's neck. Micah held her at the waist, his fingers meeting at the small of her back. He pulled Bailey more securely against him and began an easy sway. His breathing slowed as he stared down into her eyes, drowning in them.

"You don't have to be afraid anymore," he whispered.

"I'm not," she answered, but Micah knew better. He'd witnessed that type of fear before; he knew how it looked. And he hated seeing it in her eyes.

The noise of the other club goers seemed to fade away as they danced. When Bailey rested her head against his shoulder, Micah's chest tightened with such yearning he could barely breathe.

He knew it was wrong to close his eyes and imagine this was real, but he did so anyway. If he were honest with himself, he could admit that he'd been dreaming about this for weeks—months even. From the moment Bailey had sat across from him for their interview, he'd been completely enthralled by this woman. Actually getting the chance to hold her, to feel her body nestled against his, was a dream come true.

"It's been a while since I went dancing," Bailey said. "I forgot how much I enjoy it."

"Do you think you can stand to step out on the town more often?" he asked. "Not only would it help quell some of the rumors, but I think it would be good for you to have some fun, Bailey."

She raised her head and looked up at him, a small smile on her lips. "I think there may be some merit to that. As long as I'm listed as a VIP and get free food."

"I can arrange that," Micah said with a grin. After a moment, he lowered his voice and said, "Don't look now, but there's a photographer at four o'clock." Bailey started to turn, but Micah tightened his hold. He shook his head. "This is what you want, remember?"

"You're right. Let him fill up his entire memory card."

"That's my girl," Micah said. The moment the words left his mouth, he wanted to take them back. She was *not* his girl, a fact he'd had to remind himself of at least a dozen times in the past few minutes. It was dangerous to allow his mind to go that route.

Even more dangerous was the subtle smile playing across Bailey's lips as she looked up at him.

"I would have thought that spot was taken," she said. "What happened between you and the anchor from Channel 4 News? I can recall seeing you together in the tabloids quite a few times."

She hadn't looked far enough into his background to know that he'd attended Harvard, but she *had* looked far enough to know about a past relationship.

"Angelica and I are friends. Colleagues," Micah amended.

"Did things just not work out?"

"You can say that. It was never all that serious. We went to a couple of industry events together, had a few lunch dates. The only reason it made the gossip pages is because we're both local personalities."

Her brow peaked with curiosity. "So you really are single and available?"

"I'm single," Micah said. "But available is another story. You know that, Bailey."

"Is it only because of the documentary?" she asked. "Because we won't be shooting the documentary forever."

God, why did she have to remind him of that?

"Bailey…"

She tilted her head to the side, staring at him, not giving an inch.

"I already know how you feel about me," she said. "You let that cat out of the bag a while ago."

If she wanted to know how he felt about her, all she had to do was take a step closer—she'd feel it gaining life behind his zipper.

"It's okay, Micah. I don't have to be your girl if you don't want me to be."

Micah's eyes widened. "That's not what I'm trying to say. I mean, if you—"

She put her hand to his chest, laughter lighting her eyes. "I'm teasing you. Goodness, Mr. Jones. Do I need to give you lessons in how to take a joke?" She shook her head. "Look, I understand that circumstances being what they are, nothing can happen between us." She looked up at him. "But if it could…"

Micah's eyes slid closed, and a groan came from deep in his belly.

She was *killing* him.

The temptation to say to hell with propriety and journalistic integrity and all that other crap that was keeping them apart was so strong that Micah had to take a physical step back. For a number of reasons, he and Bailey just could not be together.

He opened his eyes to find her still staring at him with that sexy, vulnerable look.

"We can't, Bailey."

"I know," she said. "I'm trying to be okay with that. I guess I'll just have to try harder."

The DJ switched things up, moving from the string of ballads he'd been playing to an R & B and hip-hop mix.

"Come on," she said. "Time for me to see what kind of moves you have."

She started dancing and, for a moment, all Micah could do was stand there and watch. God, this woman was gorgeous. And sexy. The way her hips swayed from side to side—it was as if she was auditioning for a part in his nightly fantasies. She didn't need to try any harder. The part was hers. Hands down.

Apparently, all Bailey needed was this small push to get her back into party mode. They remained on the dance floor for a solid hour. The photographer he'd spotted earlier was no longer trying to hide the fact that he was catching Bailey on film, and she didn't shy away from the camera. It was fascinating to witness her in her element, living it up, having fun.

But even as she let her hair down—literally—and fully embraced everything Micah had wanted her to enjoy tonight, he remembered that there was still a threat out there. He kept his eyes open, looking for anyone who seemed to be paying too much attention to them.

Of course, that meant he also saw all the men in the club blatantly staring at her. Micah couldn't blame them. But he had one up on them tonight—he was the one who was actually here with Bailey.

The DJ switched things up again, and Bailey tapped at her throat.

"I need a drink," she mouthed over the blaring music.

Micah nodded and led her to the bar. "You want something with a little bite to it, or not?"

"Not, please," she said.

He ordered two sodas on the rocks, then turned back to watch the action on the dance floor. At least, that was what he thought he would watch. Instead, he couldn't keep his eyes off Bailey. Her face was flushed from the nonstop dancing. Her hair had lost a bit of its bounce. And she was, hands down, the most gorgeous woman in the club. Probably in all the clubs along this stretch of the Meatpacking District, if not all of Manhattan.

She turned to him with a smile on her face. "Your friend Rafe has himself a winner here. This place is packed."

"If anyone can make this club work, it's Rafe," Micah said. He took the drinks from the bartender and handed Bailey hers.

There was a loud crash at the other end of the bar, where, from what he could tell, the other bartender had dropped several glasses. Bailey jumped so high some of the soda splashed over the rim of her glass. Just then, a guy walked up to them and grabbed Bailey's shoulder from behind.

"Hey," he said.

Bailey froze. Her eyes widened with stark terror.

Micah tore the guy's hand from her and stepped up to him. "What the hell are you doing?"

The guy put both hands up. "Sorry," he said. "I thought she was someone else."

"Something wrong?" asked a woman as she came upon them. She had wavy dark brown hair and a leather jacket similar to Bailey's.

"There you are," the guy said, and the two of them took off for the dance floor.

Micah turned to Bailey. She was trembling from head to toe, resonating with fear.

"It's okay, Bailey." He had to pry the glass from her hand; she was clutching it so tightly Micah was surprised it hadn't shattered.

He took her into his arms. "It's okay," he murmured against her temple.

Micah tightened his hold as he felt her body continue to tremble uncontrollably. He looked up and spotted Rafe marching toward them. He put a hand up, stopping his friend's approach.

"Come on," he whispered in her ear. "Let's get out of here."

Her body still shivering, she nodded against his chest.

Gone was the confident, fun-loving woman who'd spent the past hour living it up on the dance floor. She looked as scared as a cornered mouse.

Micah bit back a curse.

A night out on the town wasn't enough to cure Bailey's real problem. Neither was a few months in the Virgin Islands. She needed professional help, someone who could teach her how to properly deal with her post-traumatic issues. If she didn't address this, the abduction would continue to haunt her.

He just needed to figure out how to get her to see that.

Bailey rubbed her clutched fists up and down her thighs as she sat in the passenger seat of Micah's sedan. Her chest still felt tight, her skin tingly as panic continued to claw its way up her throat.

She was going crazy.

There was no other way to put it. An innocent case of mistaken identity, a simple touch from a stranger, and she'd nearly lost it. How was she ever going to get past this?

They pulled up to a light, and Micah's warm palm slid over her left hand. Her eyes traveled from his hand up to his face, settling on his brown eyes. The understanding and sympathy staring back at her caused her chest to tighten with something other than fear. For the moment, gratitude had taken its place.

"Thank you," she whispered. She glommed on to the comfort he offered, hating that she needed it but relishing it all the same.

"You're okay now," Micah said. "You were always okay, Bailey. Nothing is going to happen to you on my watch."

"That's just it, Micah. I don't want to be on anyone's watch," she said. "God, I'm so tired of this. I just want to be my old self again."

She'd tried so hard not to succumb to the fear that had plagued her since the attack. But it lurked around every corner, making her feel like a frightened lunatic who was afraid of her own shadow.

"Bailey, you know that you can't do this on your own, don't you?"

"Do what?" she asked.

"Get over what happened. You need professional help."

Bailey's head jerked back. Apparently, she wasn't the only crazy one in this car—he must be insane to suggest such a thing.

"Be real, Micah. The press made a headline out of me going to the dentist. Can you imagine the field day they would have if I went to a shrink?"

"Forget the press. You need—"

"What I need is to not bring any more bad press down on RHD. I've caused enough problems for my family."

"RHD is one of the most successful design houses in this city. Do you really think you seeing a mental-health professional can bring down an entire fashion empire, Bailey?" He looked at her, his eyes boring into hers. "I've seen PTSD before. It won't get better until you learn how to properly deal with it."

"I was tied up for a few hours in a basement at Lincoln Center, not captured by enemy fighters in the mountains of Afghanistan."

The light turned green, and they continued up 10th Avenue in silence for a moment.

"PTSD is not just something prisoners of war experience," he finally said, staring straight ahead.

He wasn't telling her anything she didn't already

know. After the extensive research she'd conducted online while recuperating in the Virgin Islands, Bailey didn't need some professional to diagnose her. She knew she was suffering from post-traumatic stress, but she refused to give the media any more fodder for their sensationalized stories.

Bailey pulled her hand away from Micah's.

"I'm okay," she said, proud of the resolve she was able to project in her voice, even though she didn't feel an ounce of it.

She chanced a quick glance at him as they pulled up to another red light, and his piercing look told Bailey that he could see so much more than she wanted to reveal. She'd had that feeling often over the past few days. There was something about Micah Jones. He seemed to see inside her head—a scary thought. Lately even *she* didn't want to see inside her head.

In a gentle voice, he said, "It gets better, you know. Eventually, you'll stop fearing what's behind every corner. You'll stop suspecting that every person is out to get you."

"It'll be a lot easier to stop suspecting that every person is out to get me once the person who did attack me is behind bars," she said with a vehemence that surprised her. "I'm sorry. I didn't mean to snap at you," she said.

"No. No, don't apologize," he said. "I can't imagine what you're going through, Bailey. It's not my place to tell you how you should react. You have a right to feel however you want to feel."

Silence filled the car again as they finished the drive back to her building. Micah found a parking spot only a few yards from the entrance. He got out and came around the car to open her door.

"Thank you," Bailey murmured.

He nodded, then rested his hand against the base of her spine as he ushered her inside. Bailey shut her eyes for a moment to relish the feel of his touch. It radiated a strength she could feel even through her leather jacket.

"This place is something else," Micah said as they made their way through the lobby.

"It is." Bailey nodded. They stopped in front of the elevators. "Brianna and I have toyed with the idea of moving a few times, but as you can see, we're both still here. I would like to eventually move closer to RHD. And I love SoHo—the vibe in that part of the city suits me."

"But?"

She shrugged. "This is home. It always has been. Although I wouldn't be surprised if I lost my roommate soon."

The elevator arrived. Micah motioned for her to go ahead of him. "Your sister and Collin are getting serious?"

Bailey couldn't contain her smile. "She's pregnant." She pointed a finger at him. "That does not leave this elevator. The baby is Brianna and Collin's news to break. I can't wait, though. I'm so excited about my first niece or nephew."

His lips drew up in an adorably sexy smile as he pretended to lock them and throw away the key. "No one will hear anything from me."

At this late hour, the building was quiet and the elevator's smooth ride to the tenth floor took less than a minute. When they arrived at her front door, Bailey debated whether or not to ask him in for a nightcap.

He took the choice out of her hands.

"I should probably go," he said. "Believe it or not, my work isn't done. I've got a lot of notes to review for tomorrow's show."

"Why didn't you say that earlier?" Bailey asked. "I wouldn't have kept you out this late."

"I didn't mind," he said. "I enjoyed watching you enjoy yourself."

His seductive murmur sent a tremor down her spine. The air between them sizzled.

Bailey took a step forward. Micah did the same.

He ran one hand down her arm. The other went to her hair. He tucked a few wayward strands behind her ear.

"Will you be okay?" Micah asked.

Bailey nodded. "Brianna should be home by now. I wouldn't be surprised if she's waiting up for me like a worried mother hen."

"She cares about you," Micah said, his voice low and rough with something that could only be described as desire. "Nothing wrong with that."

Bailey could only nod in agreement. The knot lodged in her throat made speaking impossible. She stood still as Micah's head lowered, his eyes staring straight at her.

She sucked in a breath mere seconds before his soft lips connected with hers. Her eyelids slid shut as his mouth closed over hers. He kept things light, pressing several gentle, airy kisses against her lips. But when Bailey slipped her tongue out and touched the corner of his mouth, everything changed.

A low growl tore from Micah's throat as he wrapped his arms around her and pulled her closer, fitting her against his body. He pushed his tongue past the seam of her lips, flicking it inside her mouth, tangling with her tongue. Bailey's fingers crept up his back until they reached his head. She cradled it, holding him to her with one hand as she snaked the other up his chest. She grabbed a fistful of his sweater, clutching it as she held on to him for dear life.

After several more moments of indulging in their intensely erotic kiss, Micah pulled back. His chest heaved with labored breaths. His eyes were wide with surprise, as if he couldn't yet fully comprehend what had just passed between them.

"Uh, I should…" He pointed toward the elevator.

Bailey nodded. She couldn't speak in coherent sentences, either.

Micah gestured to the door of her apartment. "I won't leave until you're safely inside."

Her heart pinched at his compassion. He was such a gentleman.

She took out her key and unlocked the door, then turned back and gave him a wave. It seemed woefully inappropriate after the explosive kiss they'd just shared.

"Good night," she said. "I guess I'll see you later."

Micah nodded. "Good night."

Bailey looked one last time over her shoulder before she entered the apartment. She closed and locked the door behind her, shutting her eyes tight as she banged her head against the door.

"Should I even ask?"

Her eyes flew open at the sound of her sister's voice. Brianna sat on the couch, her feet tucked underneath her, a sketch pad in her lap.

"I'm in so much trouble," Bailey said.

And it had nothing to do with a crazed kidnapper. This time, she knew exactly what the danger looked like…and how it tasted.

Chapter 8

Micah sat at a right angle to George Stevens, the former director of a local children's charity who had suffered a spectacular fall from grace two years ago when he'd been caught with his hand in the cookie jar. He'd just been released from prison and was attempting to make his grand return to the spotlight. He'd decided *Connect* was the perfect vehicle with which to do so.

The poor fool.

Micah folded his hands casually in his lap, relishing showing Stevens the error of his ways.

His interviewee stared at him with so much hate in his eyes that a lesser man would have cowered. But Micah could hold his own with the best of them. He continued with his relentless questioning.

"You represented the most vulnerable demographic in this city—underprivileged children. Did you once think about the people you were supposed to help, and how they would feel once your treachery was uncovered?"

Stevens sat back in his chair and pressed his steepled fingers against his lips, biding his time before answering, "At the time, I believed I was doing what was best for the children."

"You believed using donations for personal vacations was the best use of the funds collected for the poor inner-city youths your charity served?"

"I considered those trips research."

Micah flipped through the sheaf of papers his production assistant had provided just before they went live. He needed a minute to calm himself down before he threw professionalism out the window and punched the hell out of George Stevens.

"During an eight-month span, you visited Bora Bora, the Florida Keys and Maui. Exactly what type of research were you conducting?"

"It was for a new playground that I commissioned."

"A playground?" He had to fight hard to keep the smile from his face. His job shouldn't be so damn easy.

By the time the hour ended, George Stevens looked as if he'd gone ten rounds in the boxing ring, and Micah was reminded of why he loved his job so much.

At the end of the show, Stevens refused to shake Micah's hand; he and his handlers stormed away from the set. They were not given much sympathy from the *Connect* crew.

"That was some of the most entertaining television I've seen in a while," Ben said.

"The guy served two years in jail and still refuses to admit he's a thief," Micah said as he unhooked his mic. "I sure as hell wasn't going to take it easy on him. That's the problem with people in the public eye today. They're used to getting coddled instead of facing hard-hitting questions."

He handed the audio equipment to the production assistant and frowned at the sly smile that drew across his cameraman's face.

"What?" Micah asked.

"I guess Bailey Hamilton is lucky you don't take that same attitude toward models."

Micah's head reared back. "What's that supposed to mean?"

"I'm just making an observation."

"And I'm just asking exactly what it is you think you've observed."

Ben shrugged. "You're shooting a documentary on a fashion model who was found clutching a bag of co-caine, but you haven't mentioned that once. Some people may think that you're taking it easy on her, especially after the way you just handed Stevens his ass."

"I'm not taking it easy on Bailey," Micah protested. But even as he said the words, Micah knew they weren't entirely true. He *had* been treating her with kid gloves, but that was only because he knew the full story—or at least more than the rest of the media knew.

Ben held his hands up. "Like I said, just making an observation."

Micah watched the other man as he continued toward the break room. He fought the urge to follow him so he could try to make a stronger case—if he protested too much, it would likely backfire.

Instead, he headed for his office, shutting the door behind him, and collapsed into his chair. He was exhausted, and his body was starting to rebel from the lack of sleep.

Micah folded his hands over his chest and leaned his head against the headrest of his ergonomic chair, a gift from his mother when *Connect* had launched. He closed his eyes and tried not to think for just a minute, but it was no use.

At the forefront of his mind was, as usual, Bailey. But not for the reasons she had taken up residence in his psyche over the past two months. Now whenever Micah thought about her—which, granted, was way more than he probably should—his thoughts were shrouded with guilt over the turmoil he had inadvertently created for her.

He would give up his home, his car, everything he owned, if he could go back in time and change that interview. Why hadn't he considered that his questions could jeopardize her safety?

But how could he have known someone would use the information to hurt her? He had interviewed hundreds of guests over the course of his career. Nothing like this had ever happened before.

And now he had something else to worry about. The idea of Ben believing that he was biased toward an interview subject didn't sit well with him. The thought of his professional integrity being brought into question made Micah's stomach churn with unease.

What was even more unsettling was that he'd thought it himself more than once over these past couple of weeks, especially after that kiss last night.

What the hell had I been thinking?

He hadn't been thinking—that was the problem. He had been dying to kiss her since the interview, and last night he'd finally had his chance. The minute he saw desire reflected in those enchanting brown eyes, he'd been done for. Utterly, completely done in by those exquisite lips, that sensuous body, her beautiful, gentle soul.

God, he was falling hard for her. But he wasn't just falling—he was tumbling headfirst without brakes, barreling toward that *L* word he'd managed to steer clear of for the past thirty years.

"Damn it," Micah cursed, running both hands down his face.

He knew better than this. He couldn't allow his emotions or his libido to override his common sense.

A knock at his door jarred him from his musings.

"Come in," Micah called.

Jessica Silverman, who produced the evening news program, stuck her head into his office.

"Rebecca's called for a quick meeting. She wants to discuss the new lineup," she said. She put a hand up. "And before you ask, yes, *Freshmen Escapade* is still included." Rolling her eyes, she closed the door.

He and Jessica were on the same page when it came to the reality show that had been proposed by Rebecca Barrington, another of the station's producers, and the one person who could give Micah a run for his money over the executive producer position. He and Rebecca had vastly different visions of where to take the station. She wanted WLNY to ride the wave of reality-TV shows that thrived on drama-filled ridiculousness. *Freshmen Escapade*—which was slated to start in the spring, following four New York college freshmen as they learned more about partying than schoolwork—was just one of Rebecca's stellar ideas.

She'd also hounded him about getting whatever dirt he could find on Bailey. Rebecca wanted to turn his documentary into the same kind of sleazy programming she wanted to bring to the rest of the network's lineup.

Micah wanted the station to get back to covering substantive issues. When he'd first started at WLNY, the lineup had been filled with thought-provoking programming that actually made people think. *Connect* was now one of the only shows that continued in that tradition. Micah wanted to bring the station back to its former glory, not tear it down with shows about partying college freshmen.

He checked his email and phone to make sure he didn't have anything pressing, and couldn't suppress his disappointment at not seeing anything from Bailey. He shouldn't be upset; they weren't scheduled to meet again until tomorrow. But that didn't lessen his disappointment.

When Micah arrived at the small conference room where their cable station's meetings were normally held, the other segment producers were already there, along with Mark Davis, the general manager.

Mark motioned for Micah to take a seat, then said, "Before we get started discussing the spring lineup, I want to know how things are going with your documentary, Micah. Can we expect to run it during the holiday sweeps?"

Micah nodded. "Roger Hamilton Designs is holding a special fashion show next week. That will be the final day of filming. We've been editing as we go, so I expect the finished product to be done within the next couple of weeks."

"Is the dirt you're getting on Bailey Hamilton filthy enough to schedule this in the Sunday night prime-time slot?" Mark asked.

"I heard that she was seeing some psychiatrist to the stars," Rebecca piped in.

"Look," Micah said, intentionally ignoring Rebecca's comment and forcing himself to stay as calm as possible at the disrespectful mention of Bailey's mental health. "There is no dirt on Bailey Hamilton. This documentary is going to show how RHD has helped to make her a rising star in the fashion industry. It's about family, and how having a strong support system can lead to success."

Every person in the room just stared at him. Even Jessica was looking at him as if he'd grown two heads.

Rebecca cut the silence with a sharp laugh. "You're joking, right? Tell me you're joking, Micah."

"No, I'm not joking," he gritted out.

"You have an exclusive with the person at the center of one of the juiciest stories to hit New York this year, and you're going for the wholesome-family angle?"

"The Hamiltons *are* a wholesome family," he said.

"It's inspiring what they've been able to accomplish while holding their family together."

Mark Davis was shaking his head. "Not this time. Rebecca is right. The drug scandal with Bailey Hamilton is what people what to know about. That's what you need to focus on."

"I promised Roger Hamilton that I would not turn this into some sordid, sensationalized story," Micah argued.

"You lied," Mark stated. "Now let's turn to the lineup for the spring season."

Micah seethed with barely contained anger as he sat back in his chair, pretending to listen as each producer rattled off ideas for the upcoming season. What he really wanted to do was get up and walk out, with a parting request for each and every one of them to kiss his ass.

He didn't care what Mark said. He was not going back on his word to the Hamilton family. He couldn't do that to Bailey, especially now that he knew the truth about her supposed drug scandal.

God, how he hoped they caught the man behind her attack. For one thing, Bailey's world would be a hell of a lot safer if her kidnapper was no longer on the streets, but just as important, she could clear her name.

Micah finally understood the frustration the Hamilton family had been suffering these past few months, knowing that Bailey had done nothing wrong yet having to witness her reputation being dragged through the mud. To this day the rumors about her continued to spread.

But Micah would be damned before he added to

them. He didn't care what Mark or Rebecca wanted, nor did he care about the executive producer position. He would walk away from the project and the promotion before he turned Bailey's documentary into a smear fest.

"So are you adding cameraman to your résumé?" Bailey grinned. She stretched her arm over her head, angling her body to the right.

She sat with her legs crossed, in the common yoga pose that he'd already forgotten the name of. As if he could concentrate on the names of the poses she'd been twisting her body into for the past half hour in Central Park. It was taking every ounce of restraint he possessed not to reveal just how much watching her bend and flex in those skintight exercise clothes turned him on.

"I can operate a camera when the time calls for it," Micah answered. "I interned at a station in Boston as an undergrad. I was required to learn every part of the process."

He'd chosen to shoot this morning's session using a classic 8-millimeter camera. The vintage-looking footage would be incorporated into a montage of different snippets of Bailey doing everyday things. His creative self was getting excited at the thought of the montage.

Another part of him was getting excited for an entirely different reason.

Bailey closed her eyes and pulled her hands down in front of her. Micah watched, mesmerized, as her chest rose and fell with several deep breaths. Her eyes opened and another of those smiles graced her lips. He'd gotten way too used to those smiles over these past few weeks. He wasn't sure how he would ever live without them.

"This is the first time in months that I've exercised in the park," she said.

They'd found a perfect spot in the park, not too far from her building. It was chilly, but the direct sunlight hitting their little patch of grass made it comfortable.

"How often would you come out here?" he asked, the camera still rolling.

"A couple of times a week. I typically exercise at the gym, simply because it's more convenient, but getting out here and breathing in the fresh air never fails to relax me."

"We haven't really discussed the lengths you have to go to in order to keep in shape," he said. "It's a sticky subject in the fashion industry, isn't it?"

She shrugged. "Of course body image is a huge deal. The nature of this job is to put yourself out there so that people can judge your appearance. But it isn't everything. I want to show people, especially young girls trying to break into this business, that there is more to modeling than just a pretty face and a tiny waist. I've seen too many girls fall for that."

"How did you manage not to get caught up in the body-image trap?"

"I've always had a healthy amount of self-esteem. I suspect it comes from being the baby of the family, and having everyone dote on me." She chuckled. "As you can probably tell, I use it to my advantage all the time."

Once, Micah would have argued that her self-confidence was one of her best assets, but in the weeks since she had returned to New York, he'd perceived more insecurity and self-doubt than anything else. Her family had to have seen it, too, but they were all more concerned about not upsetting Bailey. What everyone failed to realize was that continuing to ignore the real issue was likely to cause more harm than good.

She finished up her yoga routine and they walked over to a newsstand at the 72nd Street entrance for something to drink. She gestured to the ice-filled trough in front of the stand and Micah shook his head, declining her offer. He shut off the camera and, after she'd made her purchase, pointed to several tabloids that had pictures of her, all with unflattering headlines.

"How does that feel?" he asked.

"Seeing my face plastered across the papers?" Another shrug. "I've gotten used to it."

The headline—What Is Bailey Hamilton Hiding?— was printed in bold red ink above a picture of her heading into a coffee shop. Designer sunglasses covered her eyes and she was clutching her coat closed at her throat. He'd been there the day that picture had been taken. He knew she wasn't hiding anything—she'd simply wanted a hot chocolate.

At that moment, Micah felt ashamed to be in the media. Bailey hadn't asked for this scrutiny, yet she couldn't even step into a coffee shop without the press putting some type of salacious spin on it.

He was about to apologize yet again for his role in the havoc that had been wreaked in her life when Bailey's cell phone rang. It was a call from her future sister-in-law, telling her that she was needed at RHD. Micah had mentioned wanting some shots of her at home to show her more personal side, so she invited him to come up while she showered and changed.

He spent the five-minute walk to her Central Park West building trying like hell to calm the desire raging in his blood. Watching her nimble body twist and arch during her yoga routine had pushed his control to the limit. Maintaining that control as she stripped naked and got slippery wet just a few yards away from him was asking too much.

As they rode the elevator up to her floor, Bailey filled Micah in on the building's history, but his mind refused to concentrate on anything but thoughts of her soon-to-be-naked body.

They entered the apartment and, after making sure the door was locked behind them, Bailey tossed her keys in an oblong silver dish on a table next to the door.

"I won't be long," she said. "Help yourself to anything in the fridge."

He wanted to help himself to *her*.

God, this was killing him!

Micah cleared his throat, trying to break free from the lust that was nearly choking him. "I'm going to shoot the apartment," he said. He focused his attention on the framed photographs on the mantel. "Is anything off-limits?"

After a moment's pause, she answered with a soft, sensual, "No."

The invitation Micah perceived in that single word caused him to whip around.

Bailey stood just inside the arched entrance to the

hallway that led deeper into the apartment. Her eyes were full of the same raw desire that had been building in his bloodstream all morning.

Micah pitched his head back and groaned at the ceiling.

"Bailey, please don't make this any harder for me." He looked over at her and nearly lost the battle to keep his hands off her. His throat ached, but he pushed past the pain and said, "I can't."

"I know," she answered. "But for the record, I don't agree—I think you can."

Then she turned and headed for the back of the apartment.

Micah let out the breath that had seized in his lungs. He needed to leave this place right now, before he made the biggest mistake of his entire career by gaining carnal knowledge of an interview subject. If he allowed that to happen, he could kiss what little impartiality he had left goodbye.

But he still had work to do.

So instead of leaving, Micah fired up his 8-millimeter and started filming. Viewing the apartment through the lens of his camera gave him the distance he needed from the situation, in addition to greater insight into how Bailey and her sister lived. They both apparently loved bold colors—there was not a pastel to be found. The decor matched what he knew of both Hamilton women's personalities.

A narrow glass-topped buffet table was lined with framed photographs of Bailey and her siblings, along with pictures of her surrounded by young girls in front of a Boys & Girls Club of New York banner.

One thing Micah found odd was the fact that there was not a single picture of Bailey modeling. She must have posed for thousands of high-fashion portraits over the years, but there were no stills of her in the middle of a bold strut down the runway, or of the many magazine ads she'd appeared in.

Micah came upon a display case of figurines that looked similar to the ones his mother had inherited from one of her former clients. The collection was his mother's pride and joy—after her only son, of course.

"I didn't peg you as someone who would be interested in Lladró pieces."

Micah turned at the sound of Bailey's voice. "Is that what they're called? My mom has a bunch of them."

"Your mother collects Lladró?"

"She does now," Micah said. "She's a home health nurse. One of the women she took care of left her collection to my mother. You would think she'd inherited the moon."

"Depending on which pieces she has, she may have. I've been collecting these since I was a little girl."

"Do you want to see her collection? She would get a kick out of showing it to someone who actually knows what Lladró is."

"I would love that," Bailey said. Then she turned to him and, crossing her arms over her chest, asked, "So are we going to talk about that kiss the other night, or are we just going to pretend it never happen?"

Her boldness shocked the hell out of him. Micah had

been creeping around that tinderbox since Friday night, waiting for that ill-advised kiss to blow up in his face. After a few days had gone by without Bailey mentioning it, Micah had hoped the subject would just magically go away.

Not that it had stopped him from thinking about it.

Bailey put a hand up. "Never mind. I think I already know your answer."

"Bailey—"

She shook her head. "It's okay."

"Not really," he admitted with a humorless laugh. "Look, what happened outside the door of your apartment on Friday was not one of my more professional moments."

She folded her arms again. "Lack of professionalism aside, are you sorry it happened?"

Nothing within him would allow Micah to tell that lie. "No," he said. He pinched the bridge of his nose and expelled a frustrated breath. "That kiss gave me life, Bailey. You have to know that."

Her expression softened, and a small smile lifted the corner of her mouth. "I do," she said in a gentle voice. "It did the same for me."

The urge to pull her into his arms was so all consuming that Micah couldn't remember ever wanting anything more.

"I told you from the very beginning that I'm attracted to you, and that attraction has only grown stronger these past few weeks." With a sigh he admitted, "Every second I'm around you is a struggle."

Her forehead dipped into a frown. "You say that as if it's a bad thing."

"It is. The way I feel about you goes against my code of professional ethics, but being around you and not touching you kills me. You know that I want you."

"Then why are you fighting it?"

"Because you don't need me wanting you right now. Bailey, you have so much that you're dealing with—that you *still need* to deal with. Getting involved with me would only complicate your life."

"So now you know what's best for me, too? When did you add psychologist to your résumé?"

"This is serious, Bailey. It's not a game."

"I know it isn't a game," she said, stepping up to him. Before he could stop her, she linked her hands behind his head and pulled his face to hers. "It's very real. And it's happening. Stop fighting it."

The precious little fight he had left in him was no match for the ardor that Bailey brought to the kiss. With the first lick of her soft, wet tongue against his lips, Micah's will to protest was completely annihilated. He wrapped his arms around her waist and tugged her against him. Then he went for her pliant lips, melding them to his own.

He slipped his hands underneath her sweater and caressed her spine, his skin pebbling with goose bumps of desire as his fingers grazed the silky fabric of her bra. Micah brought both hands around and cupped her silk-and-lace-covered breasts. As Bailey's nipples hardened beneath his palms, his erection did the same, pushing against the fly of his pants.

A soft moan escaped her lips. The sound washed over him, urging him on, driving him to push his tongue deeper, knead her breasts harder, press himself more firmly against her belly. Micah licked and sucked her tongue, pulling it into his mouth, relishing her flavor.

Bailey's hands trailed down his back to his backside. She grabbed his ass, clutching him to her middle.

His body lit up like a bonfire.

Micah picked her up and took the couple of steps to the sofa. He laid her across it and covered her body with his. As he pressed his straining erection to the hot warmth between her legs, he trailed his tongue down her throat. Then he pushed her sweater up, past the tops of her breasts, exposing the full, luscious lace-covered mounds. He tongued her protruding nipples through the lace, bathing them with long, wet licks before sucking them into his mouth.

Bailey clutched his head to her breast while her hips undulated underneath him. Micah thrust against her, rubbing his rock-hard erection back and forth, the friction fueling his pleasure.

Bailey arched her back and her body stiffened as she cried out toward the ceiling.

"Oh, my God," she let out with a deep breath.

Micah lifted his head from where he'd buried it against her neck. "I can't believe I just dry humped you in the middle of your living room."

A giggle bubbled up from Bailey's throat. "God, that felt good," she said.

Guilt tried to creep up on him, but that satisfied look on Bailey's face beat it back. Her contented smile was worth any bout of self-reproach he would eventually suffer.

Micah pushed himself up with shaky limbs and sat on the far end of the couch. Evidence of his unfulfilled orgasm bulged against his fly.

"I would offer to take care of that for you, but you would just bring up that journalistic integrity thing," Bailey teased.

Micah leaned his head back against the sofa, covering his eyes with one arm while the other fell into his lap. He felt Bailey shift on the sofa.

"Don't," he warned. "You need to get to RHD."

"Is that the best excuse you can come up with?"

"And I need to go to the station." Micah took a chance and looked at her. Just as he'd anticipated, his body responded by growing even harder. "I'm trying to do the right thing here, Bailey."

"The right thing for who?"

Micah dragged a hand down his face. He needed to get out of here before he said to hell with his conscience and carried her to her bedroom.

"Why don't I pick you up from RHD? We can take a drive into Brooklyn and you can see my mom's figurine collection."

"Bringing up your mother at a time like this? Nicely played, Mr. Jones." She laughed, then said with an exaggerated sigh, "If that's all you're offering, I guess seeing your mother's Lladró collection will have to do."

He looked over and had to stop himself from reaching out to her.

"I wish I could offer more, Bailey."

"So do I," she said.

Micah considered giving into the impulse to kiss her one more time, but he didn't trust himself to stop at just one kiss. Instead, he grabbed his camera from the side table and got out of there before he could do something else he would later regret.

Chapter 9

"Hey, where's your shadow?"

Bailey turned at the sound of Daniel's voice. "Who?" she asked.

His brow arched in amusement as they boarded the elevator at RHD. "Don't even try it. You know who I'm talking about." Daniel playfully tugged her hair, bringing the big-brother routine to an annoying level. "He follows you around like a lovesick puppy," he teased.

Bailey could feel the blush creeping up her neck. She swatted her brother's hand away. "I thought you hated Micah."

He shrugged as they got off on the fourth floor and walked toward the brainstorming room to which they'd both been summoned.

"I'll be the first to admit that in the beginning I was ready to kill the guy, but he's started to grow on me.

And he's damn good at his job," Daniel said with a fair amount of respect.

Bailey was rendered momentarily speechless. Daniel didn't mete out praise often, and he tended to be particularly harsh when critiquing others in his profession. It said a lot about how much Micah had grown in Daniel's esteem these past few weeks.

Evidence of just how much Micah had grown on her entire family became even more apparent as Bailey, her mother, Brianna and Zoe sat around the conference room table, looking over the box of favors that had just been delivered for Zoe's wedding shower that coming weekend.

"How are things going with Micah?" her mother asked as she fluffed the netting around the wedding bell filled with candied almonds.

"Okay, I guess," Bailey answered with a shrug. "He refuses to let me see any of the raw footage but promises that he'll have a rough copy for me by the end of next week. Once we're done with the resort-wear show, he'll be able to put the finishing touches on it."

"I'm not talking about the documentary," her mother replied.

Bailey looked up to find her mother regarding her with that shrewd, knowing look she'd perfected through years of dealing with her children. Brianna and Zoe were mimicking that same look.

"What?" Bailey asked, sounding overly defensive.

"Oh, give it up, Bailey," Brianna said. "We want to know what's going on between the two of you."

"Nothing's going on," Bailey said, picking up another favor.

"Something is definitely going on," Zoe said. "Or if it isn't yet, it will be soon. Everybody sees how that man looks at you."

Bailey's eyes shot to her future sister-in-law. "How does he look at me?"

"The way Kyle looks at me," Zoe said with a laugh.

If the attraction pulsing between her and Micah was this apparent, Bailey wasn't sure she wanted her family to see the two of them together after what had happened a few hours ago on her couch. A shudder flowed through her body at the recollection of the magic his tongue had wielded.

Oh, God! I can't think about the man's tongue with my mother sitting next to me!

"We're going to see his mother later today," Bailey said. Six eyebrows arched in surprise, and she quickly added, "She collects Lladró figurines. When he found out about my obsession, he told me he'd bring me over to see her collection."

"Hmm…that sounds serious," Brianna commented. "Meeting the mother."

Bailey rolled her eyes. It was probably pointless to try to hide her and Micah's involvement outside of the documentary, but she wasn't ready to share just yet.

"Do you have everything you need for the shower?" she asked Zoe.

"I met with the event planner earlier this morning. She's coming by later today with cake samples. I guess you won't be able to give your opinion since you've got better things to sample," Zoe finished with a wink.

Bailey rolled her eyes again.

Kyle came into the office carting a huge box. "Did you all order everything in the free world?"

"Don't be silly. Just think of all the things in the free world," Zoe teased. She stood and planted a kiss on Kyle's lips before turning her attention to the box. "Oh, this is the fabric for Lila's dress!"

"Thank goodness it arrived," her mother said.

Zoe pried the shipping tape from the box, then flipped it open.

And gasped.

She pulled the fabric from the box, revealing silky eggshell material peppered with splotches of deep red. Bailey's blood turned to ice at the sight.

Kyle snatched the fabric from Zoe's hands. "It's dye," he quickly surmised. He turned the box over, and it was evident that it had been tampered with. The tape used to seal the bottom was completely different than the tape Zoe had peeled from the top.

"This is no coincidence," Brianna said. "Not after everything else that's happened."

Bailey whipped around to her sister. "Everything else?"

"Brianna," her mother said in a warning tone. Bailey caught the slight shake of her head.

"No." Bailey went to her mother. "Tell me what's going on."

"It's nothing for you to worry about," her mother said. "It's under control."

"Is it?" Kyle asked. "Keeping Bailey in the dark isn't going to help her. She needs to know so that she can keep her eyes open."

"What's going on?" she asked, unable to keep the hysteria out of her voice. She felt her chest tightening, felt the air restricting in her lungs. A now-familiar clamminess crawled across her palms. She sucked in a deep breath, trying to ward off the impending panic attack.

Bailey closed her eyes. "Tell me, please."

"There have been a few…incidents lately," her mother began after a pause.

"What kind of incidents?"

"In September, Kyle and Zoe were locked in a closet for several hours. The tires on his car were slashed, and we just found out that when the RHD computers crashed not too long ago, it was deliberate, the work of a hacker."

Bailey brought shaking fingers to her lips. "No," she whispered.

"We thought your abduction was an isolated incident, but it's apparent that the entire family is being targeted," Kyle stated.

"Why am I just hearing about this now?" Bailey demanded. Her body was shaking with something other than fear—she was furious.

"You've been through enough already," Brianna said. "You didn't need this on top of everything else."

"Stop treating me as if I'm a piece of glass," Bailey snapped. "I'm not going to shatter at the first sign of trouble. I deserve to know what's going on in this family, too."

There was a knock on the door. Bailey turned to find Micah poking his head through the slightly opened door.

"Am I interrupting something?" he asked.

"No," Bailey said. She stalked out of the conference room, grabbing her jacket off a chair. "Come on. Let's get out of here."

Micah looked at Bailey out of the corner of his eye as they moved in a sluggish crawl across the Williamsburg Bridge into Brooklyn. He adjusted the car's heating vents, then chanced asking a question.

"You want to talk about whatever has you ready to pound your fist through my windshield?" he asked.

She shook her head, but seconds later said, "Apparently, others in my family have been through troubling episodes lately. Incidents, as my mother called them."

"Such as?"

"Someone slashed the tires on Kyle's car and hacked the computers at RHD. And today the fabric for my mother's dress for the wedding arrived covered with red dye. The box had been tampered with." With a derisive snort, Bailey said, "My family thought it was too much for my fragile brain to take, so no one bothered to tell me."

Micah was torn between feeling enraged over yet another incident against the Hamiltons and relief that they had finally clued Bailey into what had been going on. It had been weighing on his mind ever since Brianna had told him before he'd taken Bailey to Rafe's club.

"Someone is targeting your entire family," Micah stated. He gripped the steering wheel in an attempt to control the rage coursing through him. The thought of anyone getting their hands on Bailey again made him crazy.

"And it all started with me. This is all my fault, Micah. If I had been paying attention that morning—"

"No." He cut her off. "Don't you see, Bailey? It's the exact opposite. Who's to say they weren't after Kyle? Or someone else in your family? This isn't just about you."

Her eyes registered comprehension, as if she had never considered that she might not be the cause of the reign of turmoil being wreaked upon her family.

"This isn't your fault, Bailey."

She expelled a tired sigh. "I'm just ready for it to end," she said. "I'm ready to get my life back."

"You will. Just let the police do their job. They'll eventually find out who's behind this. And in the meantime, remember there are people looking out for you. Your family was just trying to protect you. They don't want any more harm coming your way. Neither do I."

He reached across the console and covered the hand that was resting on her thigh. She flipped her palm up, and her elegant fingers twined with his, closing tightly. She gave his hand a squeeze, and Micah felt it in his chest. She had no idea of the hold she had on his heart.

As they drove toward his mother's home, Micah pointed out buildings and places he used to visit while growing up.

"We lived over there, in the Bushwick-Hylan projects," he said, pointing to the housing development where he'd grown up.

"Did you go to school here?" Bailey asked, pointing to a building in the next block.

"No, I went to Stuyvesant in Manhattan."

"Stuyvesant?" She twisted in her seat and stared at him. "Do you know how tough it is to get into Stuyvesant? At least twenty thousand students apply every year, and they only accept the top five percent."

"Actually, it's more like the top two percent."

She laughed, then said, "You're a smarty. Stuyvesant, and then Harvard?"

Micah looked over at her, one brow cocked in inquiry. "Is being a smarty a good thing or a bad thing?"

"Definitely a good thing," she said. "I find intelligence very sexy."

It felt as if the car's temperature had climbed twenty degrees. Micah knew he was playing with fire by encouraging the seductive banter, but he told himself that it was for Bailey's own sake. He was taking her mind off the incident that had happened back at RHD. Yeah, that was what he was doing.

He pulled up to the curb in front of the brownstone where his mother now lived, near Irving Square Park. It wasn't anywhere near as nice as the building that housed the Hamilton clan, but compared to the one-bedroom apartment in the projects where he'd spent most of his childhood and teenage years, it was a palace.

His mother greeted them at the door.

"Hi," Bailey said, putting her hand out. "I'm Bailey Hamilton."

"No introduction is necessary," his mother answered.

"I'm Rochelle Jones. It's so exciting to meet you. I see your face on TV all the time."

Micah shrugged. "I guess it's no big thing that my face is on TV all the time."

"Oh, come in here, you," his mother said, batting his arm.

She led them into the house. Micah glanced over at Bailey, surprised to realize he'd been expecting to find derision on her face as they stepped into his mother's modest home. He should have known better. He was standing next to the most gracious, down-to-earth woman he'd ever met. Even if she *had* been put out by the house, Bailey never would have revealed her feelings. She was much too polite.

Her face lit up the moment her eyes found his mother's Lladró collection.

"Well, I can tell what you're here for." Rochelle gestured to the shelves of figurines.

Before his mother could join Bailey, Micah pulled her in for a hug and placed a kiss on the top of her head.

"How's it going?" he asked. "You know that's code for 'What do you have to eat?' right?"

That garnered another playful tap on the arm. "There's leftover sweet-potato casserole in the refrigerator."

"Oh, God, how I love you," Micah said with another quick kiss before he jetted for the kitchen. He dished up a plate of his mother's famous sweet-potato casserole, which he usually didn't get to eat until Thanksgiving. Evidently Thanksgiving had come a week early this year.

When he returned to the living room, he found his mother and Bailey oohing and aahing over the figurines.

"I am so jealous," Bailey said. "Do you know how hard it is to find this piece?"

"I've had it for years. And before you even ask—no, you can't buy it."

"How did you know that was my next question?" Bailey said with a laugh.

The sound traveled across Micah's skin, leaving a ribbon of sensation in its wake.

"How unfair is this?" Micah said, stepping into the room. "I would get pinched whenever I got too close to these when I was a kid."

"That's because you wanted to blow them up with your Transformers," his mother returned.

"This collection is one of the most complete I've ever seen," Bailey said. "I'm in awe."

"It's my pride and joy."

"Next to your only son," Micah added.

Rochelle pointed to the plate in his hand. "How's the casserole?"

"Delicious as usual."

"Bailey, would you like some sweet-potato casserole?" his mother asked. "Oh, wait. You're probably not allowed to have that as a model."

Bailey slid her a look. "Says who? A sweet potato is a vegetable, right?"

His mother threw her head back with a laugh. They all filed into the kitchen and his mother dished up a hefty serving of casserole for Bailey.

"I'll be back in a minute," his mother said, excusing herself from the kitchen.

A knowing grin drew across Bailey's face as she stared at him.

"Good?" Micah asked, nodding to the casserole.

"Wonderful," she said. "So is your mom. She's so down-to-earth."

"She's probably thinking the same things about you."

His mother returned to the kitchen carrying two leather-bound binders.

"I've taken up a new hobby. Scrapbooking!" She placed the binders on the table. The first was filled with pictures of her and a group of girlfriends who had taken a trip to the Bahamas over the summer.

"We want to visit either Jamaica or the Virgin Islands next year," Rochelle commented.

"The Virgin Islands are beautiful," Bailey said.

"Oh, which ones have you visited?"

Bailey looked up at her. "Most recently St. Thomas, but I've been to several over the years. It's usually where Roger Hamilton Designs shoots its swimsuit collection."

The next scrapbook had Micah wishing for a meteor to fall from the sky and put him out of his misery. His mother had apparently found every single embarrassing picture ever taken of him, from butt naked in the bathtub as a toddler to sporting cornrows during his high school years.

She and Bailey pointed and laughed while Micah plotted ways to get his hands on the book and burn it.

"This one is from Halloween. He wanted to dress like a witch because he was convinced girls got more candy."

"I was four," Micah deadpanned, shaking his head as Bailey wiped tears of mirth from her eyes.

His mother patted his hand. "I'm sorry. We're not laughing at you, Micah—we're laughing *with* you."

"That would be true if I were laughing," he pointed out. But then he ruined his annoyed look by grinning.

"Oh, I completely forgot about the Egyptian pieces," his mother said.

Bailey's eyes lit up. "You have the Lladró Egyptian collection?"

"Not all of them, of course, but a few. I keep them in a special lighted display case."

She pointed Bailey in the direction of the dining room.

As soon as she was out of hearing distance, his mother turned to him.

"I'm so happy you brought her over, Micah. You know I've wanted to meet her since she appeared on your show. She is just as charming in person as she was during your interview." With a cagey smile, Rochelle added, "She also seems to be very comfortable with you." Micah instantly recognized that glint in her eyes.

"Don't," he warned.

"What?"

As if he was buying the innocent act.

"Bailey is the subject of a documentary I'm producing. That's all she is. Don't try to make anything more out of it."

"Hmm, funny how you've never brought any other *subjects* here."

Micah pitched his head back and let out an exasperated breath. "Don't," he said again.

Bailey came back into the kitchen and Micah shot his mother another look.

"We should probably be getting back," he said. "I need to go into the station for a bit."

A lie. He needed to get his mother away from Bailey before she got any ideas about campaigning for a daughter-in-law. She had only barely tolerated most of the girls he'd dated. But Micah could see the wheels turning in her head with Bailey.

Bailey smiled at his mother. "It was wonderful meeting you, Rochelle. Thank you so much for sharing your Lladró collection. And the pictures." She turned back to Micah and with laughter in her eyes said, "You'd better make sure she keeps those under lock and key, because if someone ever wanted to blackmail you, that's all the ammunition they would need."

After more laughter at his expense, they made their way out of the house, his mother following them to the car. Micah opened Bailey's door for her and waited for her to get in, then gave his mother a kiss on the cheek before bidding her farewell.

"Your mother is lovely," Bailey noted as they turned onto Knickerbocker Avenue.

"Thanks," Micah said. "That woman is my world."

"Has it always been just the two of you?"

He nodded. "She and my dad divorced when I was still an infant. She tried to keep in contact with him for my sake, but he was never really interested. Doesn't matter," he said. "She did enough to fill both roles. She's one of the strongest women I know."

"She's proud of everything that you've accomplished. You really are a testament to what you can do when you work hard and want it badly enough."

"And you're not?" he asked as they pulled up to a red light.

"I didn't have to work that hard. I was born into my lifestyle."

"Don't do that, Bailey. Don't discount what you've accomplished simply because you were born into privilege. You've worked hard to get where you are, too. You should be proud of that."

She was quiet for a moment, a contemplative look on her face. Finally, she acknowledged, "You're right. I had to work my way up the ranks of RHD just like the other models. In fact, I sometimes think I had a harder time because my dad didn't want anyone accusing him of nepotism. I *have* worked hard." She looked over at him, and with a gentle smile said, "Thank you for reminding me of that, Micah."

Her voice was thick with emotions that he tried to parse. There was gratitude, but there was something else in there. Something he could sense just underneath.

Desire? The same kind of want rushing inside his veins?

A car horn honked behind them. Micah glanced in the rearview mirror and continued along the boulevard. By the time they arrived back at RHD, the building was nearly deserted, with only a few designers still hunched behind their massive computer monitors or draping fabric over headless mannequins.

Micah followed Bailey into the break room, accepting the can of soda she offered him.

"Thank you for today," she said.

"Are you kidding? My mother loves showing off her figurine collection. I should thank you for being so enthusiastic about it."

"That's not what I was talking about," Bailey stated. "I know what you tried to do today, and I appreciate it."

Micah didn't deny it. He took a step forward and fingered the lock of hair resting on her shoulder. "You needed to get your mind off what happened. I'm happy I could help."

Mere inches separated them. Micah stood there, mesmerized by the pulse beating at the base of her throat. Her distinct scent reached his nose, imbuing his brain with everything that was good about her.

Bailey closed the distance between them. Her eyes shut as she tilted her head up.

"I should go," Micah said, releasing her hair and taking two pronounced steps back.

The crestfallen look that crossed her face made him feel like the worst person in this universe and the next, but Micah knew his limits. If he remained here just a few seconds longer, he wouldn't be able to resist her.

He couldn't help reaching out and trailing a finger down her cheek, though. "I'll see you later," he said before turning and walking away.

Chapter 10

"What do you have planned for tonight?" Brianna asked as she stood before the mirror in the living room. She slipped on a pair of turquoise earrings to match her turquoise-and-brown sweater dress.

"Probably just hanging out here," Bailey said. "After all that time doing nothing in St. Thomas, you'd think I could go a year without watching another made-for-TV movie, but I just want to veg out for the rest of the night."

"Of the two of us, I definitely have the better plans for the evening," Brianna said with a wink.

"Whatever." Bailey rolled her eyes but laughed. She could never begrudge Brianna for the fun she was having. Seeing her sister so happy had been one of the highlights of being home these past few weeks.

"When are you and Collin planning to let the rest

of the family know about the little bun in the oven?"
Bailey asked.

"Collin is ready to let the world know, but I don't
want our news to take away from Kyle and Zoe's wedding."

"It won't," Bailey assured her. "There's no such thing
as too much good news, especially right now."

"I guess you're right," Brianna said. "Hey, don't wait
up for me. I'm spending the night at Collin's, so I won't
be back until the morning. If you need anything—"

"I have a building full of fiercely loyal protectors just
waiting to rush to my rescue. Don't worry about me,
Brianna. I'll be fine."

"Good. I know I don't have to tell you to lock up after
me, but I'm telling you anyway."

Her sister kissed her cheek before leaving the apartment. Bailey couldn't help but follow what had become
her usual routine, checking several times to make sure
the door was locked, and then going around the apartment checking all the windows, even though she'd done
so just a few hours ago. Clearly, she had moved past run-
of-the-mill crazy to downright insane, but she couldn't
stop until she knew every lock was secure.

She went into the kitchen and eyed her cell phone
on the counter, trying to decide if she really had the
gumption to go through with the plan she had devised
earlier today.

"You can do this," she said, picking up the phone and
calling Micah before she lost her nerve.

"Hello," he answered in his deep, smooth voice.

"Micah, it's Bailey," she said. "I was wondering if

you could come over. I had a couple of things I wanted to discuss about the documentary. After seeing your mother's Lladró collection, I thought maybe I could describe a few of my pieces on camera. It would be a way to humanize me."

"You don't need to be humanized," he argued.

"That's debatable, but I'd still like to add it to the documentary if we can."

She heard rustling, then Micah said, "Give me about an hour."

She disconnected the call and sucked in a deep, reassuring breath. One hour. That was how long she had to set up the seduction.

Bailey groaned. "You are out your mind," she said, cradling her head in her hands.

She was no seductress. She would be lucky if Micah didn't laugh in her face.

Bailey picked up the phone, intending to call him back, but forced herself to put it down.

She could do this. She *wanted* to do this.

She'd finally found someone who saw more than just the fashion model, someone who was able to look beyond the glitz and glamour to the real woman she was inside. She wanted to show him every part of her.

Bailey looked down at her slacks and turtleneck sweater. Her ensemble was as appealing as a cactus to bare skin. She took a quick shower and changed into a persimmon-colored loungewear set. It was decent enough to be worn outside the house, but the lace trim around the V-neck bodice gave it a hint of sexiness.

After spritzing a bit of Brianna's fragrance at her

wrists and behind her ears, she looked herself over in the full-length mirror.

"Not bad." She twisted and looked over her shoulder at her rear end. "Not bad at all. And not too desperate." She didn't want Micah to walk in and know right off the bat that she was planning on seducing him.

The doorbell rang, and Bailey nearly jumped out of her skin. Now that the time was here, what little confidence she'd convinced herself she felt was melting away like a polar ice cap in the desert.

"You can do this," she said, taking a deep breath.

Bailey called on that inner strength she used when striding down the runway as she walked across the living room to answer the door.

"Hi," she said, reminding herself to breathe as she stared at Micah.

"Hi," he answered. "Can I come in?"

"Oh, yes, of course," she said, moving out of the way so he could enter the apartment. "Good show," she said. She gestured to her television when he looked at her with a curious arch to his brow. "I DVRed your show with the former director of that children's charity."

"Oh, yeah."

Bailey frowned at his lackluster tone. "What? You don't think it went well?"

"No, the interview was fine. I accomplished what I set out to. But…"

"But?" she asked when he didn't continue.

Micah expelled a frustrated sigh. "Someone accused me of being harder on George Stevens than I've been on some other guests."

Bailey caught the subtle suggestion in his voice and the lightbulb went on in her head. "Like…me?"

He nodded.

"*Have* you been taking it easier on me?"

"Bailey, you know my objectivity goes out the window when it comes to you. Do you think I take all of my guests out to a club, or to visit my mother?"

"If I had to guess, I'd say the answer is no."

"You would be right." He ran a hand down his face. "This is the kiss of death in my line of work. Impartiality and journalistic integrity is everything. No one will take me seriously if they believe I'm taking it easy on you because of…well…other reasons."

"And those reasons would be?" she asked.

The heated look in Micah's eyes told her everything she needed to know, and Bailey suddenly realized that this seduction would be much easier than she'd first anticipated.

He started to answer, but she put a finger to his lips and whispered, "Show me."

Bailey saw the moment the fight went out of him. His eyelids closed and he pulled her to him, slipping a hand behind her neck and tilting her head up. The minute their mouths met, Bailey's knees went weak. She grabbed on to Micah's shoulders, fearing her limbs wouldn't be able to hold her up as he unleashed an onslaught of sensual passion on her. She opened her mouth and drew his tongue inside, gently sucking it, savoring the taste.

Micah wound his arms around her and pulled her in close, crushing her chest against him. He walked them to the sofa and sat, pulling Bailey on top of him so that her legs straddled his hips. All the while their mouths continued to dance.

Bailey reached between them and tugged his shirt from his waistband, then tunneled her hands underneath and splayed her palms against his solid chest.

She trailed one hand down to his zipper and cupped the growing erection she found there, squeezing it, teasing it, marveling at the way it grew bigger and stronger underneath her hand.

Micah let out a groan as he pumped his hips up, reaching for her touch.

Then he stopped short, catching her wrist.

"Where's your sister?" he asked.

A smile pulled at the corner of Bailey's lips. "She's at Collin's tonight."

"All night?"

She nodded. "All night."

"Thank God," he said, then he pulled her to him again. Their tongues jousted as their hands continued to explore each other. Micah pushed her shirt up and wrapped his fingers around the sides of her waist. Bailey finished the job, pulling the top completely off and tossing it onto the floor.

The heat that shone through his hooded eyes caused an instant blush to rush along her skin. She could only imagine the picture she created, straddled across his lap in her sheer black bra. Micah leaned forward and flicked his tongue across one nipple and then the other. The erotic picture her breasts must present, swollen and wet from his tongue, caused moisture to pool between Bailey's legs.

"Micah, please," she pleaded, unsure of what she was asking for, but knowing that she needed *something* more to happen. *Now.*

"What is it you want me to do?" he whispered against her throat as his fingers plucked and pinched her nipples through the thin fabric.

"Let's go to my bed," she said.

He pulled away and stared at her. His eyes were filled with so much fiery desire that Bailey felt it on every inch of her skin.

Micah pushed them both up from the sofa. He wrapped her legs around him and cradled her butt in his hands as he took them the few yards to her bedroom. Once there, he let her fall back onto the bed, immediately following her and heading yet again for her breasts. He lowered the cups of her bra, freeing her breasts from their sheer barrier. While he sucked on one nipple, he used his fingers to pinch and rub the other.

Bailey held his head to her chest with one hand while the other, of its own volition, traveled down her stomach and into the waistband of her matching sheer black panties. Her fingers rubbed back and forth across the swollen nub of nerves pulsing at her cleft until it tightened unmercifully.

"That's *my* job," Micah whispered against her neck as he pulled her hand away and replaced her fingers with his own. He teased her clitoris, flicking his thumb back and forth across it as his middle finger dipped inside her. Her body instantly clutched around him, pulling his finger deeper inside.

The bevy of erotic sensations drove Bailey to the edge. Her stomach tensed as the orgasm began to build. She tried to stanch the desperate moans climbing up her throat, but it was no use. It had been too long since she'd done this—she couldn't hold back.

Micah sucked hard on her nipple and she let out a sharp gasp. She was on the brink of exploding. *Almost there. Almost.*

Bailey's head pitched back as she screamed, her body convulsing as the tremors of release coursed through her. After several moments she floated back down to earth. Her limbs were weak and trembling, her entire body humming with sated relief.

Micah pushed himself up and knelt on the bed between her spread legs. Bailey thought he was about to finish undressing, but instead, he drew his hands down his face and said, "We shouldn't go any further, Bailey."

Oh, no. No, no, no.

She would die if he walked away from her right now. She needed him to fulfill the promises he'd made with his hands and tongue.

"Micah, don't do this. Please, don't walk away from me."

"I should," he said.

Bailey closed her eyes, her entire being recoiling at his words. She bit her trembling bottom lip, and tried like hell to keep her emotions in check.

"But I can't."

Her eyes popped open as his softly struck words registered.

"I know I'm crossing the line here, Bailey, but there's no way I could leave you in this bed. Even if it's just for one night, I have to have you."

He climbed off the bed and slowly, deliberately released the buttons on his shirt. Bailey crawled to the edge of the bed and helped him tug it off his broad shoulders. She went for his undershirt, but he caught her wrist and shook his head.

"I've got this." He jerked his chin toward the bed. "Go."

She did as he commanded, sliding back until she was resting against the headboard.

Micah pulled his undershirt over his head, then dropped it on the floor with his other shirt.

Bailey's eyes were instantly drawn to the narrow trail of hair that started at his navel and disappeared into his waistband. She wanted to trace her tongue along that path until she found the treasure awaiting her behind his zipper.

Anticipation had her breath coming out in audible pants, though Bailey could barely hear it past the thumping of her heart within the walls of her chest. With every garment he discarded, the pulse between Bailey's legs beat harder and harder.

Micah drew his wallet from his back pocket and retrieved a gold foil packet. He tossed the wallet on the nightstand, and the condom to her. Bailey caught it in both hands and tore the package open. Then she returned her eyes to the show.

He unbuckled his pants, and with the same deliberate slowness, drew the zipper down. He hooked his hand in his waistband and pushed the pants down his legs. He stood there in a pair of black boxer briefs— RHD boxer briefs.

Bailey pitched her head back and laughed. "Did you wear those for me?"

He nodded, and she laughed again. But then her eyes narrowed into slits. "Which means you had intentions of letting me see your underwear," Bailey said in an accusing voice.

"It was wishful thinking."

"Well, now that your wish has come true, I'm ready to see you *without* the underwear."

A sexy grin tilted the edge of Micah's lips as he shoved the last piece of clothing from his body.

Goodness. He was *magnificent*.

Every inch of him was practically perfect, from the way his skin shone over the firm muscles of his arms and legs to his tight washboard abs. But Bailey was shamelessly drawn to his impressive erection. She needed to get that inside her as soon as possible.

Micah climbed onto the bed and knelt between her spread legs. He took the open packet from her and pulled the condom out, rolling the slippery latex over his erection. Then he caught her hips and pulled her toward him. With a look of hunger in his eyes, he splayed his fingers over her inner thighs and stretched her legs apart. With one deep plunge, he entered her body.

Bailey's eyes closed and her hands went to his chest. As Micah drove his thick, firm erection into her with deep, insistent thrusts, Bailey massaged his flat nipples until they grew into hard peaks. She lifted her head and traced her tongue down the column of his throat and along his collarbone. Micah nudged her head up and covered her mouth with his, thrusting his tongue inside, matching the rhythm of his hips as they continued to pump over and over.

"God, Bailey, you're killing me," he breathed against her lips.

Without leaving her body, he flipped them over, planting her on top.

A moment of self-consciousness tiptoed up her spine, but Bailey dismissed it when she caught the passion and desire in Micah's eyes.

With a reverence that stole her breath, he tenderly drew his fingers over her body, trailing them along her sides, cupping her breasts, rubbing his thumbs in gentle circles around her nipples.

Levering himself up on one elbow, he lifted his head and drew her nipple into his mouth, then quickly switched to the other, going back and forth as his right hand traveled down. He clasped her hips and guided their rhythm as she rode his lap, her body undulating, moving faster and faster as that sensation she'd felt before began to build low in her belly once again.

Bailey braced her hands on Micah's chest, rolling her hips again and again. And when Micah reached down and rubbed her throbbing clit, her entire world exploded. Her back bowed as she shouted toward the ceiling. Her limbs trembled as wave upon wave of pleasure crashed through her, rendering her speechless, unable to do anything but collapse onto Micah's strong chest.

Moments later, his body stiffened and he came with a ferocity that left them both breathless.

Micah pulled Bailey closer against him, taking pleasure in the feel of her moist skin against his own. Yet even as he fitted her body to his, he knew he needed to step away.

He couldn't even count how many ways he'd violated the ethics he'd pledged to adhere to as a journalist. Not only had he taken advantage of Bailey while she was the most vulnerable, he'd knowingly disregarded the numerous warnings in his head. He knew this was wrong. Yet it hadn't stopped him.

"You're frowning."

Micah looked down to find Bailey's brown eyes staring up at him from where she lay on his chest.

"Bailey, you know we shouldn't have done this, don't you? I can't even explain how wrong this is."

She stretched her entire body over his, rubbing her leg against his steadily hardening erection. Micah fisted the satiny sheet in his hand in an attempt to bring his body under control. It wasn't working.

"You can say that, even though your body is saying otherwise?"

He blew out a weary breath. "I didn't say I didn't want to do it. I said we *shouldn't* have."

"You can still be impartial, Micah. What we did tonight doesn't change that."

He looked down at her. "Are you serious? Do you

really think I can be objective after the things I did to your body tonight? Do you think I can ever look at you again as just work?"

Bailey shook her head. "But you can't go back and undo it," she said. "So, please, don't ruin what happened with regrets. Tonight was too beautiful for it to end with either of us regretting it."

Micah pushed a lock of hair behind her ear and caressed her cheek. As he stared into her eyes, he couldn't help falling deeper under the spell she continued to weave around him.

"No, I can't undo it," he said. "And I don't want to. I know I crossed a line tonight, Bailey, and I'll eventually have to deal with the consequences. But, given the chance, I would do it again in a heartbeat."

A shy, beautiful smile graced her lips, but when it turned wickedly sexy, Micah knew he was in trouble. Bailey climbed on top of him, straddling his waist again.

"Well, here's your chance to do it again," she said.

So he did.

Hours later, Micah lay across the bed on his stomach, his arm draped over Bailey's middle. He wasn't sure how long he'd been awake, just watching her. The moon cast a gentle glow over them, bathing Bailey in a mellow light that made the light brown streaks in her hair shine like gold.

Even as part of him knew that this was the dumbest move he could have possibly made career-wise, another part—the part he chose to listen to now—was content to just lie there and bask in her exquisiteness. Micah was still unable to fully comprehend that he was in Bailey Hamilton's bed, that he'd made love to her over and over just hours ago. She had occupied his fantasies for so long that the reality of it was hard to believe.

She'd insisted on putting on a nightgown after they had both decided that they would die if they made love again, and he couldn't help but tease her over her shyness. She was one of the most beautiful, sexy, photographed women in the country. She'd graced the covers of magazines and strolled confidently down the runways of New York, Paris and Milan, yet she had been self-conscious about remaining nude in bed with him. Micah was fascinated by the contradiction.

He moved closer to her, wrapping his arm more firmly around her middle, and nuzzled his nose against that spot just below her ear. It had driven her crazy earlier. Maybe he could do the same now.

Bailey stirred, but she didn't wake up.

Micah nuzzled some more, while his hand inched down to her ridiculously smooth thigh. He fingered the edges of her lace-trimmed baby-doll nightgown, then pushed it up past her waist.

Just then, a loud boom crashed outside, like a garbage truck hitting a pothole.

Bailey popped up, her eyes bright with panic. She scrambled out of the bed.

"Bailey!" Micah lunged for her but missed.

She ran to the door and locked it, then flattened her back against it. Her chest was heaving with deep breaths.

Micah turned on the lamp next to the bed, then cautiously approached her at the door. In a hushed voice, he said, "Bailey, it's okay." Her eyes shot to his and widened, as if she hadn't realized he was there. "It's okay," he repeated. "It was just a truck on the street. Nothing is going to hurt you."

Understanding dawned in her luminous brown eyes, followed by horror and shame. She covered her face with her hands as she slumped against the door.

Micah gathered her into his arms and pressed a kiss to her temple.

"It's okay," he said over and over again, smoothing his hand down her hair and along her spine. Her body trembled, and no matter how tightly he held her, Micah couldn't get her to stop shaking.

"You must think I'm crazy," she said against his chest.

"You're not crazy, just afraid. It's okay to be afraid, Bailey." Micah cradled her cheeks in his palms and lifted her face to his. "But you don't have to live this way for the rest of your life. You can get past this."

"I'm trying," she whispered.

"I've seen it, Bailey. I know you can get past this with the right help. My mother, she was in your shoes once."

She looked up at him and his heart lurched at the panic still shimmering in her brown eyes. Micah pulled her closer, wishing he could take away her pain.

"My mother was in a relationship with a man who beat her," he continued.

"But I—"

"I know it's not exactly the same scenario, but there are similarities. The fear I see in your eyes... I saw it in my mother's all the time. She tried to pretend that everything was fine for my sake, but even as a kid, I could tell it wasn't. That fear paralyzed her, but eventually she got out of that relationship and, in time, she stopped being afraid.

"You can get past this, too, Bailey. But you first have to acknowledge what the kidnapping did to you."

She shook her head. "I'm over it."

"No, you're not. God, Bailey, how can you not see that? You're practically climbing the walls because of a truck driving down the street." He brushed away the remnants of her tears with his thumb. "It takes more than just telling yourself that you're okay. You need to take the necessary steps to actually get to a place where you're no longer afraid. You can't get there on your own. You need help."

"The press would have a field day with that, Micah, and you know it."

"Someone stole something from you that day. He stole your peace of mind. You deserve better than to live your life in fear."

"I'm not—" she said, but he cut her off, placing his fingers over her lips.

"You are, but I swear I'll help you, Bailey. All you have to do is let me."

"Do you really want to help me?" she asked.

He nodded. "More than anything."

"This is all you have to do," she said. She cradled his head in her palms and pulled his mouth to hers. Micah knew this was a defense tactic, a way to shut him up so that she didn't have to deal with the real problem.

It worked like a charm.

Chapter 11

Bailey stood with her hands above her head as her sister draped the maxi-dress fabric around her.

Brianna peered up from where she was crouched at Bailey's waist and, holding a pin between her lips, mumbled, "You know you're glowing, right?"

Bailey tried to affect a look of confusion. "What are you talking about? You're the pregnant one. You should be glowing. Now hurry up so we can get over to the hotel to help with the setup for Zoe's bridal shower," she said, trying to change the subject.

Her sister just continued to stare with a knowing grin.

Bailey's shoulders slumped. And here she thought she was doing a good job of concealing her recent trip to cloud nine. "Is it that obvious?"

"The only thing that would be *more* obvious is if you

wore a T-shirt with 'I just had an orgasm' spelled out in hot pink rhinestones."

"Brianna!" Bailey's face instantly flamed.

Her sister nearly choked she was laughing so hard. "Just stay away from Kyle," she said. "If he sees that blissful look on your face, he'll probably attack Micah."

"Oh, God," Bailey groaned. That was all she needed, her overprotective brothers becoming even more over-protective.

"So?" Brianna wiggled her eyebrows. "Was he any good?"

Bailey barked out a laugh. "Um, let's just say his talents extend beyond television."

Daniel, walking into Brianna's office without both-ering to knock, interrupted their laughter. He was fol-lowed by their cousin Nelson, who looked mad enough to kill.

"Uh-oh," Brianna said, "what's going on?"

"People suck," Nelson said.

"Care to elaborate?" Bailey asked.

Daniel lifted the cover on the candy dish Brianna kept on her desk and scooped up a handful of M&M's. He gestured toward their cousin before popping a few into his mouth.

"Nelson found out that he wasn't the Hamilton that the producers of his reality show were really interested in. They wanted Bailey."

"Me?" she yelped.

Nelson nodded. "That's the only reason I was hired. They were trying to get closer to you."

"What did they expect you to do?" Brianna asked. "Strong-arm Bailey into being in the show?"

"Everyone knows how close the Hamilton family is," Nelson said. "They figured you wouldn't turn down your own cousin."

"Sorry to break it to you, but I would have," Bailey told him.

"I never would have asked in the first place," Nelson said. "I don't want to ride someone else's coattails. If they don't want me for me, then they can shove their job up their—"

"Just be careful," Daniel said, cutting Nelson off. "I know I don't have to tell you that there are some in the media who would do just about anything to get a story out of you, Bailey."

"I know," she said. "I'm not stupid."

"No one said that you were."

"I'm also not some naive first timer who doesn't know how this business works," she added. "I've been at this long enough to know when I'm being used."

Even as she said the words, uncertainty needled her brain. She hoped that she was savvy enough to read someone's intentions, but she also knew how adept people could be at hiding their true selves. Being part of the fashion world all these years, she'd seen her share of the fakeness that resided just underneath a shiny veneer.

Daniel and Nelson left the office and Brianna got back to work, doing the last-minute touch-ups on the designs that would be modeled in that week's fashion show.

"Oh, crap," Brianna said. She covered her mouth with

her hand. "I've bypassed morning sickness and moved on to all-day sickness." She dropped the pincushion and took off for the bathroom.

Bailey grinned, thinking about the new addition to the Hamilton family. Brianna was going to make a great mother, and Bailey couldn't wait to be the very cool aunt who spoiled her niece or nephew rotten.

A few hours later, Bailey followed Brianna into one of the smaller banquet rooms at the Childs International Hotel, where Zoe's wedding shower was being held. The room was breathtaking, just like the rest of the hotel. Two giant crystal chandeliers hung from the ceiling, their glittering lights reflecting off the raw-silk-covered walls. Three-foot-high centerpieces towered above round tables draped with linen.

Bailey spotted her mother, who had long since taken over preparations for Zoe's wedding shower, even though it should have been Bailey and Brianna's job as bridesmaids. Lila Hamilton was in her element directing workers on where to place things.

"This looks amazing," Bailey said, greeting her mother with a peck on the cheek.

"Thank you. I figure it's a dry run for the wedding."

"What can I do to help?" Bailey asked. And, as anticipated, her mother put her right to work. A half hour later, she was sprinkling iridescent glitter along the edges of the head table when her mother walked up to her.

"Where's the cake?" she asked. "It should have been delivered over an hour ago."

Bailey shrugged. "I thought maybe you were holding it in the back until the start of the shower."

"The shower starts in under an hour. Maybe the caterer knows where it is."

Two workers carrying an ice sculpture resembling intertwined hearts entered the banquet room. "Where should this go?" one of them asked.

"I need to handle this," her mother said.

"Don't worry about the cake," Bailey told her. "I'll find the caterer."

She went in search of the woman who had been to RHD several times over the past few weeks, bringing in food samples for both Zoe's bridal shower and the upcoming wedding.

"Melissa?" Bailey called when she spotted the woman directing the staff on where to place the covered serving trays. Bailey pointed to the table where the cake should have been. "Did the bakery call to say they were running behind with the cake?"

Melissa's brow dipped into a frown. "Not that I know of. I wasn't in charge of the cake. Zoe wanted to use a bakery that I don't contract with."

Bailey called Zoe, who was still at home getting ready for the shower.

"Is something wrong?" Zoe asked.

"They're probably just stuck in traffic," Bailey said, not wanting to alarm her future sister-in-law. "I'll just call to find out how far away they are."

But even as she said the words, an uncomfortable feeling traveled up Bailey's spine. She tried to brush the feeling off as being overly dramatic, but she couldn't shake the sense of foreboding that had the hair on her neck standing on end. Too much had happened over the past few weeks.

When Bailey called the bakery, her intuition was confirmed.

"Please tell me you're lying," she said.

Her mother picked that moment to return to her side. "What's the matter?" she asked.

Bailey held up a finger and said to the person on the other end of the line, "Well, have you any idea who called?"

Bailey's eyes closed. She ended the call with the bakery, her stomach churning with dread.

"What's going on?" her mother demanded.

"Someone—" She cleared her throat. "Someone cancelled the order for Zoe's cake."

"What?"

"The bakery said they received a call two days ago from a woman claiming to be Zoe Sinclair. She told them she'd found another bakery and she wanted to forgo the deposit she'd paid on the cake and cancel the order."

"Zoe picked that bakery because she wanted them specifically. She said she'd been using them for years."

"I know," Bailey said. She looked at her mother. "This is not just a coincidence, is it?"

The consternation on her mother's face told Bailey all she needed to know.

"Oh, my God. This is crazy!" Bailey said. "What could I have done to piss someone off so much that they would attack my entire family?"

"Don't you dare blame yourself for this, Bailey. None of this is your fault." Her mother took her hands. "This didn't start with you, Bailey. It started before you were ever kidnapped. Whoever is behind this had the entire family in their sights from the very beginning. I'm convinced of that."

Micah had maintained the same, convinced that Bailey's abduction was just one in a number of planned attacks against her family. At this point, it didn't matter who was the target of this reign of terror. Bailey was ready for it to end.

When Zoe arrived at the hotel, she was understandably upset. They continued with the shower as planned, but the atmosphere was strained. Once the guests were gone, the entire Hamilton family huddled in Collin's large office at the hotel. Even though the bridal shower had been a women's-only affair, their father, Kyle and Daniel had all come to the hotel after their mother called to tell them about the cake.

Zoe suggested that they postpone the wedding, but that idea was immediately shot down. She rattled off the list of awful things that had happened to the Hamiltons over the past few months, but Bailey's mother was adamant. There would be no postponing.

"The Hamiltons do not cower," her mother said. "We're not going to stop living our lives because of this."

The police had been called and informed of the incident with the cake. They assured the Hamiltons they would contact the bakery immediately to try to gather information on the call that had been made a few days ago.

Bailey knew it was a long shot. Whoever was behind this had been careful enough and clever enough not to leave behind a shred of evidence when he'd kidnapped her. He'd most likely used an untraceable phone when he'd called to cancel the cake.

Bailey stopped short. A streak of alarm raced down her spine as a thought occurred to her.

The person from the bakery had said that it had been a *woman* who'd called pretending to be Zoe. If this was connected to her kidnapping, as everyone now suspected it was, then they had all neglected to consider that the perpetrator was not acting alone.

As the family dispersed from Collin's office, Bailey pulled Brianna to the side. "Do you think the police are looking for the right person?" she whispered under her breath.

"What do you mean?"

"The person I talked to at the bakery said it was a woman who called to cancel the cake."

Confusion furrowed Brianna's brow, but then understanding shone bright in her eyes. "But you said it was a man who kidnapped you, right?"

"As far as I can remember," Bailey said. "It all happened so fast, and whoever it was hit me from behind. I never got a clear look."

"But could a woman have carried you to that basement?"

"I don't know," Bailey said. "Maybe whoever abducted me is working with an accomplice, or maybe he just paid some random woman off the street fifty bucks to call the bakery and cancel the cake order. There are so many possibilities."

"And way too many questions," Brianna said. "Whoever is doing this knows details about the inner workings of RHD, Kyle and Zoe's wedding, even which bakery Zoe likes to use."

"And they have it in for our family," Bailey said.

Fear pulsed through Bailey's bloodstream. Whoever was behind these attacks had proved they were willing to commit a felony to get their point across. The question was: What point were they trying to make?

And just how far were they willing to go to make it?

Micah stood to the right of the runway that extended from the arching band shell of Lincoln Center's Damrosch Park. It was the site of RHD's resort-wear show, and the place where Bailey had been abducted less than three months ago. He tried to tell himself that he was being unreasonable, but Micah couldn't shake the feeling of dread filling his stomach.

He did not want Bailey out on that runway tonight, not after what he'd witnessed just a few minutes ago.

The normally cool and collected Lila Hamilton had been distraught over the news that her future daughter-in-law's wedding dress had gone missing from the studio of the close friend who was designing it. An hour after the dress had been reported missing, it was found draped across the hood of Kyle's car in the parking garage adjacent to RHD, ripped to shreds.

If anyone still had any doubts, the picture was now

undeniably clear: the entire Hamilton family was the target of something sinister.

As Micah observed the crowd of photographers, reporters and other fashion-industry people gathering inside the white tent that had been erected in the park, he couldn't help but imagine one of them as the person who'd assaulted Bailey. This was more than likely the same collection of people who'd been here during Fashion Week. Any one of them could have snatched her that fateful day. Any one of them could be waiting to complete the job they'd started back in September.

What the hell was Bailey trying to prove by intentionally putting herself in harm's way again? That she was over her abduction? That she'd somehow won?

It was complete bullshit.

She wasn't over it. The abduction still haunted her, no matter how much she tried to hide it from the rest of the world. Micah could see just how much it still affected her whenever they were together. A trace of that anxiety lurked behind every smile.

Bailey was of the mindset that if she told herself she was okay enough, eventually it would become reality. But Micah knew better. And the only thing stepping out on that runway tonight would prove was that she didn't take her safety nearly as seriously as she should.

"I don't like this," he heard just over his shoulder.

Micah turned and found Daniel Hamilton standing a few feet behind him, his eyes zeroed in on the crowd.

"It's dangerous and unnecessary," Daniel said.

"So why the hell are you all allowing her to do this?" Micah asked him.

Daniel shot him a cynical scowl. "You've been following her every step for nearly a month. Do you think
you can stop her?"

Micah bit back a curse, pissed because Daniel was
right. If Bailey wanted to do something, there was not a
person on earth who could stop her. And unfortunately,
she was hell-bent on doing this.

"There's more security here than they would have
for the pope," Daniel reasoned, as if trying to convince
himself. But that didn't matter to Micah. He wasn't in
love with the pope.

He was in love with Bailey.

He'd known for days, but had finally accepted it after
leaving her apartment the other morning. He'd fallen
half in love with her before she'd walked off the set of
Connect in September, and the feeling had blossomed
since her return to New York. He couldn't imagine
going back to a time when she wasn't in his life.

He had to talk to her. At least one more time. He had
to convince her not to step onto that runway, because
something in his gut told him that she shouldn't go out
there tonight, and he trusted his gut above all else. It
had never steered him wrong.

Micah's purposeful strides took him to the dressing room behind the band shell in under a minute. He
rapped on the door.

"Bailey, I need to speak with you."

When she didn't immediately answer, he knocked
again, preparing to barge through the door if she didn't
open it in the next three seconds.

"Bailey!" he hollered.

The door swung open. Bailey stood on the other side, wrapped in a silk robe that stopped just above her knees.

Micah was immediately hit with a wave of lust. Coupled with the adrenaline and fear that had started pumping through his bloodstream before she answered the door, it was enough to almost bring him to his knees.

"We have to talk," Micah said. Without waiting for an invitation, he entered the dressing room and took her wrist, tugging her with him to a back corner.

"The show starts in less than a half hour, and Suzanne still hasn't finished my face. I don't have much time, Micah."

"Don't do this, Bailey."

"What do you mean? Don't do what?"

"The fashion show. You shouldn't do it. It's too dangerous."

She took a step back, her features contorting with indignation. "I am not backing out of the show," she stated.

"Bailey, with all the things that have happened to your family these past few months, it would be insane for you to go out on that runway. The person who kidnapped you could be out there right now." He pointed toward the door. "Why would you walk right into his hands again?"

"The person who kidnapped me could have been out there at every show that I've ever done. We may never know. And there are more than two hundred people in that audience, Micah. Do you honestly think someone could kidnap me in front of all of them?"

"Someone could shoot you," he said. Her head jerked

back as if she'd suffered a physical blow. "Did you ever think about that, Bailey?" Micah pressed.

"There are metal detectors," she said. "My dad insisted on them."

"All the precautions in the world won't stop someone who's determined to hurt you. Whoever is doing this is stepping up the pace of the incidents. It could all crescendo into this guy doing something unthinkable to you tonight."

After a pregnant pause, she huffed out a laugh and crossed her arms over her chest. "You watch too many cop shows."

"This isn't funny, Bailey."

"No, it's not," she said, her voice taking on an edge. "It's ridiculous, and a waste of my time." In an accusatory tone, she asked, "What's the real reason behind this?"

"The real reason? I just told you. I think—"

"You've known about this show for weeks, yet now you think it's dangerous? Is it really my safety that you're concerned with, or losing your exclusive?"

Micah's head reared back. *"What?"*

"It's not as if it's a secret that having the Bailey Hamilton exclusive has been important to your career. You said it yourself. And I've learned just what lengths people in show business will go to in order to get what they want. Just ask my cousin Nelson."

"Nelson? What the hell does Nelson have to do with this?" Micah could hardly keep up with the conversation.

"He discovered that the producers who hired him

only did so to get closer to me. They wanted to capital-
ize on my story."

"Bailey, do you really think I give a damn about
some news story? We're talking about your life here."

"Exactly. It's *my* life." She put her hands on her hips,
her chin rising as she took several steps closer to him.
"I've spent my life listening to people tell me what to
do, and I'm done with it. I'm expected on the runway in
twenty minutes, and nothing you, my brothers or anyone else says or does will stop me."

She spun around and walked back toward the van-
ity, where her makeup artist—who had been watching
them with a wide-eyed look on her face—resumed Bailey's makeup. Micah just stood there, feeling powerless.

What could he do? He couldn't tie her up and keep
her from going out there, even though that was beginning to sound like a viable option. He was pretty sure if
he brought the idea to her brothers, he could convince
both Kyle and Daniel to help him.

Micah shook his head, clearing away the ridiculous
thought.

Bailey was determined to go through with this. All
he could do was watch and pray that it wasn't something
they all lived to regret.

Bailey stared in the bathroom mirror, her hands
clutching the sides of the sink. The attack had hit with
blinding speed, sending her into a maelstrom of panic.
Blood rushed to her ears, the pounding deafening and
growing louder and louder with each second that passed.
Her chest constricted with anxiety, snatching the breath

from her lungs. She was light-headed and so dizzy with fear that she was afraid she'd collapse if she let go of the sink.

"Everything is okay," she muttered past the panic clogging her throat. "Everything is fine."

But everything was *not* fine.

She wished she could blame Micah and his irrational claims about her kidnapper possibly being in the crowd, but Bailey knew exactly where the blame lay. She had not been fine for months. And no matter how much she'd tried to tell herself that things would eventually get back to normal—that *she* would get back to normal—she knew that she was getting worse. And she would not get better until she got help.

"Damn it." She shut her eyes tight and concentrated on taking deep, calming breaths. "You're going to be okay." Bailey repeated the statement over and over until the tightness in her chest and her grip on the sink loosened.

She looked intently at the reflection staring back at her. She couldn't go on like this. She could not allow these episodes to define her existence. And she didn't have to, if she got the help Micah had urged her to look into.

There was a knock at the door. "Bailey, are you okay? It's almost time."

"I'll be out in a second, Brianna."

She grabbed a tissue from the box next to the sink and gently dabbed at her eyes, careful not to damage any of Suzanne's work. Pulling in another deep, fortifying breath, Bailey stepped out of the bathroom and found Brianna waiting on the other side of the door.

"The place is packed," her sister said, grabbing her hand. "And they're all waiting for you. You ready to give the crowd what they want?"

Bailey squeezed her sister's fingers. "I am *so* ready."

The excited buzz from the crowd was palpable—Bailey could practically feel it on her skin. It had been her idea to have the lights dimmed and the stage and runway in total darkness. The temperature inside the tent had been gradually lowered to match the frigid temperatures outside.

The crowd was hit with an extra blast of cold air as the lights came on and the winter scene was revealed. A roar of approval echoed in the tent and the first models strutted onto the stage, dressed in one-piece bathing suits.

Bailey stood at the base of the steps that led to the stage. She removed her robe and adjusted the cups on her fuchsia-and-black bikini. Her bottom half was covered in the matching sarong.

At Brianna's signal she climbed the stairs and walked through the opening in the winter-white curtains.

The fear and trepidation Bailey had experienced just a few minutes ago were completely gone the moment she stepped onto the runway. The audience went wild, their applause and roars of approval urging her on, reminding her of everything she loved about her chosen career. This was her calling.

And, oh, my God, how good it felt to be there again. With her chin high and her chest thrust forward, Bailey strutted across the stage with her signature walk, the fabric of the silky sarong fluttering with her movement. She stopped at the predetermined marks along the runway to pivot and pose for shots. Once she reached the far end of the runway, she released the knot at her hip and shook the sarong loose. The crowd roared again. Flashbulbs went off, creating sparks of dancing lights around the tent.

Bailey did several more turns before starting back up the runway. When she got to the middle, she peered over her shoulder, and with a sly, seductive smile on her face blew a kiss. The crowd loved it. Bailey hooked the sarong over her shoulder and strutted toward the curtains.

She owned this stage, and everyone in the room. Tonight was what the Fashion Week show should have been. Tonight was all about Bailey Hamilton, and she was loving every minute of it.

The minute she got off the runway, she was bombarded with hugs.

"That was awesome, Bailey! Way to steal the spotlight," another model said with a good-natured laugh.

Her mother ran up to her and cradled her face. "You were amazing."

"I learned from the best," Bailey said.

"Okay, okay, we can all celebrate after the show," Brianna snapped, in full work mode. "Bailey, maxi dresses are next. Don't forget the straw hat and sunglasses."

Bailey didn't even mind her sister's bossy tone. In

fact, she relished it. *This* was normal. *This* was what had been missing these past few months.

Finally, it felt as if things were back where they were supposed to be.

Chapter 12

"Knock, knock."

Sherrice, a junior designer, walked into Brianna's office carrying a huge bouquet of yellow, orange and deep red chrysanthemums. Bailey pushed away from the desk where she had been sitting for the past hour, reading online comments about Saturday's show.

"More flowers," Sherrice said. "These are from Manuelo. He had the delivery man tell me, repeatedly, that they were from him," she said with an eye roll.

Bailey grinned. "Are you sure they're not for you?" she asked. Sherrice had a major crush on Bailey's former stylist, and Manuelo, being the flirt that he was, teased her relentlessly about it.

His gift was the tenth she'd received in the past two days, congratulating her on her return to the runway. It was being hailed as the comeback of the year. Her cell phone had been blowing up for hours with incoming messages from friends and acquaintances. She should have been ecstatic over the abundance of praise and well wishes, but all Bailey felt was hollow inside.

Not one of the calls or texts had been from Micah.

Bailey had lost count of the number of times she'd started to call him, but what could she say? That he was right about the attack leaving her mentally scarred? That she was sorry about the accusations she'd hurled at him? That she now acknowledged that she needed a professional, but wanted his help in taking that first step?

Who was she to ask Micah to help her with anything? After the way she'd treated him Saturday night, accusing him of only looking out for his exclusive, she would be lucky if he ever spoke another word to her.

The possibility that he might not speak to her again was actually frighteningly real. He had everything he needed for the documentary. If he decided that they had nothing left to say to each other, she could very well have spoken her last words to him on Saturday night.

The anxiety that tightened her chest at that moment was a thousand times worse than anything she'd experienced during a panic attack. Bailey hadn't realized how much Micah had come to mean to her until now. In these past few weeks, he had become her definition of normal. She didn't want to think of going back to a time when he wasn't part of her life.

She loved him.

She wasn't sure precisely when it had happened, but there was no mistaking the emotion that traveled through her whenever she so much as conjured up a single thought of him.

He completed her world. A life without him was too upsetting to contemplate.

Micah stood before the door to Bailey's apartment. They hadn't spoken since the night of the show. He'd spent the majority of his time at the station, either in the editing room or holed up in his office—an office that wouldn't be his for much longer.

Micah blew out a weary sigh and hefted his messenger bag over his shoulder. His fist hovered in front of the door for a moment before he rapped on it. He could hear shuffling and then the sound of footsteps coming closer to the door. He stood up straight and stared right at the door's peephole. A second later, the door opened.

Bailey stood before him, dressed in a casual sage-colored pants-and-hoodie combination. She wore fluffy socks and her face was devoid of makeup.

She was, as always, stunningly gorgeous.

"Hi," Micah opened.

"Hello." Her voice was soft. Unsure.

He pulled in another steady breath. "Can I come in?"

She hesitated for only a moment before taking a step back and opening the door wider so that he could enter. He walked past her, caught a whiff of the scent she always wore and was nearly knocked on his ass with the need to drop everything and take her into his arms.

He walked to the living room and deposited his messenger bag next to the coffee table, then turned to her and said, "I'm sorry."

"For?" she asked.

"It wasn't my place to tell you what to do the night of the fashion show. But you have to know where it was coming from, Bailey. My fear of you going on that stage the other night had nothing to do with retaining an exclusive and everything to do with needing you to be safe."

"I know," she said.

Now it was his turn to look at her with confusion.

"Really?"

She nodded. "It was wrong to accuse you of having an ulterior motive. You're not like others I've run across in the media. You have too much integrity to use me to get a story."

Micah's eyes closed as overwhelming relief stole over him. "Thank you," he said. "Thank you for recognizing that I would *never* do anything to hurt you. Ever."

Micah wished he could just let things stand, with Bailey once again looking at him with that gentle, yearning look in her eyes. He could gather her in his arms right now. Fill his mouth with the taste of her. Fill his hands with the soft feel of her. They could forget that they'd ever fought and spend the night making love until they could no longer think.

But he loved her too much to do that.

She needed help. She would never be whole again if she didn't face her demons head-on, and the only way to face them was to acknowledge that they were there to begin with. He needed to show her how much of herself she had lost, and what was at stake.

"I have something I want you to see," he said. He

gestured for her to take a seat on the sofa, then sat next to her.

"What is it?" Bailey asked.

"Something I came across today." He slid the laptop from his messenger bag and set it up on the coffee table. Logging on to his machine, Micah pulled up the video file of the raw footage he'd run across while editing the documentary.

He turned to her and said, "Before I show you this, I need to tell you that it was Daniel's idea to add this to the documentary. You were right about insisting that he be part of this project. His input has been tremendous."

Micah pressed Play and opened the viewer to the full-screen version. The first of a number of street interviews of people voicing their opinion of Bailey started to play. Micah fast-forwarded the footage to the video that had been recorded at a school Bailey had partnered with during a mentorship program over the past year. They watched clip after clip of bright-eyed girls piling on praise and excitedly sharing what it had meant to them to work with Bailey.

A slightly pudgy, dark-skinned little girl who looked to be about ten or eleven said, "I love Bailey Hamilton because she showed me that I shouldn't be ashamed of the way I look. She told me that I am perfect just the way I am."

"I used to be embarrassed because I get a lot of my clothes from the Goodwill store," another girl said. "But Bailey told me that it doesn't matter where your clothes come from, as long as you wear them with confidence.

So now I wear my clothes with confidence and style." She struck a pose that made the other girls laugh.

So did Bailey. Micah looked over to find tears streaming down her cheeks, despite the smile that stretched across her face.

Another girl, this one with a thin, light pink scar that stretched from behind her ear to under her chin, said, "People at school used to make fun of me, but now I don't even let it bother me."

"I remember her," Bailey whispered. "She was in a car accident."

"Do you see the confidence she has now?" Micah asked. "That's because of you, Bailey. You've touched the lives of so many of these girls. You taught them how to embrace the good in their lives. You taught them how to live authentically."

Micah captured her cheek in his palm and turned her to face him.

"Every day that you hide behind that fake smile and pretend that everything is okay is a rejection of everything that you taught those girls. You owe it to them to acknowledge what that abduction did to you so that you can go back to being the Bailey Hamilton they look up to. Stop living a lie, Bailey. Get the help you need. Please."

He used his thumb to wipe away the tears that had started to cascade down her cheeks again.

"I'm ready," she whispered, and Micah's chest constricted with emotion. "I know that I need to get help," she continued. "I just don't know where to start. I don't want to harm RHD's reputation any more than I have already."

"Bailey, you're the face of the company. When people think of Roger Hamilton Designs, it's your face that pops into their minds. Talking to someone about the trauma you've been through won't change that—it will just put you back on the road to enjoying what you love. And you're not alone in this," Micah reminded her. "You have your family. And you have me. I'll be with you for whatever you need. That's my promise to you."

"What about having to be objective? Don't you think there will be talk about you being so involved with me?"

"It doesn't matter," Micah said.

"Of course it does!" Bailey insisted.

"It doesn't. Because I quit my job."

"What?"

Bailey popped up from the sofa but Micah grabbed her hand and tugged her back down.

"But how? Why? You love your job, Micah. What made you quit?"

"I could no longer go along with their vision," he said. "They wanted me to do the exact opposite of what I'd promised you and your family, Bailey. You know that sleazy, reality-TV thing your father was adamant I avoid?"

"That's what they wanted."

He nodded. "I refused to go along with it."

"So where does that leave the documentary?"

"They've agreed to air it as I present it, but it will be the last project I work on for them."

"But what about your show? God, Micah, did I cost you your job?"

"No! Don't ever think that, Bailey." He cradled her cheek in his palm once more. She covered his hand and leaned into his touch. Micah relished being with her like this. He could see himself doing so for years to come.

"The writing has been on the wall for a long time. Ever since new management took over the station." He shook his head. "I've been trying to fight it, but I'm done with the battle. I'll find something else. I've actually turned down several offers over the years. Maybe I'll call those places and see if they're hiring," he said with a laugh.

A sad smile played across her lips. "I doubt you'll be unemployed for very long. People didn't watch *Connect* because it was on WLNY. They watched it because of its host."

"Thank you," he murmured. Then he released another light chuckle. "You think your brother would be interested in starting up a production company? Turns out the two of us work well together."

"That's not such a bad idea."

"That was a joke, Bailey. Daniel and I may respect each other creatively, but he just stopped giving me the evil eye last week. We're a long way from becoming partners."

"You underestimate him," she said. "Daniel may be more inclined to work with you than you think. And, as for giving you the evil eye, he'll have to get over that if he doesn't want to end up cross-eyed, because I'm hoping you'll be around a lot more."

Micah's chest tightened with hope. "What—" He cleared his throat. "What are you saying, Bailey?"

"That I want you to be part of my life long after this documentary is complete," she said. She turned her face and kissed his palm. "I'm saying that, if you can find it in your heart to forgive me for the things I said Saturday night, that I would love to see where this leads, Micah. Are you willing to go along with that?"

"I'm willing to go wherever you want to lead me."

He took her face in both hands and brought her lips to his. Then, with a tenderness that had his limbs shaking, he laid her on the sofa and proceeded to show her just how far he was willing to go.

Chapter 13

Bailey rolled her eyes in frustration at the numbers above the elevator doors.

"C'mon, c'mon, c'mon," she muttered.

She wasn't running late. Yet. But she knew New York traffic, and with this being Thanksgiving weekend, when millions of tourists added to the millions of people who normally clogged the streets, she wanted to get to the Childs International Hotel as soon as possible. It was Kyle and Zoe's wedding day, and she wanted everything to go perfectly.

Her bridesmaid's dress had been delivered to the hotel earlier that morning. She'd just spoken to Brianna, who had assured her that she'd seen the dress with her own two eyes, and that it was unharmed. After the sabotage attempts they'd dealt with over the past few weeks, Bailey wasn't taking any chances.

The elevator finally arrived. Bailey muttered a quick, "Thank goodness," as she made it down to the lobby in less than a minute. When the doors opened, she spotted Micah walking toward her. He looked unbelievably gorgeous in his charcoal-gray suit and crisp white shirt. He wore a burnt-orange-and-gray-striped tie to match her bridesmaid's dress.

Bailey greeted him with a kiss. "You look downright edible, Mr. Jones."

The grin that lifted the corner of his mouth was pure sin. "So do you, Ms. Hamilton."

"I'm not even dressed yet," she said with a laugh. Her chuckle turned into a purr when Micah slipped an arm around her waist and kissed her. He nuzzled the spot just under her ear, pulling in an audible breath.

"And you smell amazing, as usual."

"Thank Brianna for that. She developed the fragrance."

"She can bottle that up and sell it."

"That's the plan," Bailey said with another laugh.

The doorman came up to them. "Excuse me, Ms. Hamilton, your car has just arrived."

"Perfect timing," Bailey said.

Micah led the way out of the building to the black limousine that waited under the portico.

"Good afternoon," the limo driver greeted. The woman tilted the brim of the hat that sat low above her brow.

"Good afternoon." Bailey smiled as she stepped up to the door the driver held open. As she entered the car, the woman let out a violent sneeze. "Bless you," Bailey called from within the car.

Micah climbed in and settled next to her.

When the driver slid behind the wheel, Bailey leaned forward. "The company probably already told you this, but we're going to the Childs International Hotel."

The driver nodded and, seconds later, the partition that separated the driver from the passengers started to rise.

"Excuse me, but do you mind leaving that down?" Bailey called. She looked over at Micah. "Remind me to bring up my fear of enclosed spaces when I go to see the therapist," she said.

An understanding smile drew across his lips. "I'll make a note of it." He took her hand in his and gave it a firm, reassuring squeeze.

The driver started to pull out onto the street but stopped abruptly, the car giving a vicious lurch as she stepped on the brake and suffered a round of powerful sneezes.

"I'm so sorry about that," the driver said before continuing on.

Bailey leaned back into her seat, settling against Micah. "So how is the job search going?" she asked.

"Actually, that's something I've been waiting to tell you. Did you know that your future brother-in-law's family owns a television station?"

"Childs Entertainment," Bailey said. She sat up straight. "Are you going to work for Collin?"

"I'm not sure yet, but he called me yesterday. I guess he heard about me leaving WLNY. News travels fast."

"What would you do?"

"The same thing I do now—produce, direct and host my own show. But Collin assured me that we have the same vision when it comes to content. He wants a substantive show that delves into real issues."

The driver sneezed yet again.

"Bless you," Bailey called toward the front. She turned her attention back to Micah. "It sounds like the perfect fit for you."

"I'm not putting all my hopes on Childs Entertainment," Micah continued. "Even though Collin and I know each other on a personal level, there's a possibility that things could fall through. This is business, after all. But it is definitely appealing."

Bailey threaded her arm through his. "Still, it's like one big happy family. The Hamiltons, the Childses and the Joneses."

The car jerked to the side and the driver sneezed again. Bailey sent Micah a perturbed frown. He leaned forward. "Are you okay up there?" he asked the driver.

She sneezed again. "I'm okay," she answered. "I think I may be allergic to your cologne."

Micah settled back in his seat. "Must be yours," he said to Bailey. "I'm not wearing any cologne."

A trickle of unease cascaded down Bailey's spine. She couldn't pinpoint exactly what had triggered it, but her skin began to tingle with a sense of recognition.

The driver took a left turn when she should have turned right.

"Wait a minute," Micah said. He leaned forward

again. "Ma'am, we're going to the Childs International Hotel."

The driver sneezed again.

And Bailey remembered.

Her skin became both hot and cold and dread filled her chest. "Micah," she whispered, clawing at his arm. Breathing suddenly became the hardest thing in the world. Bailey felt the blood pounding in her ears, the deafening sound of it rushing in her head.

"You're heading the wrong way," Micah was saying, but Bailey could barely make out the words. It sounded as if he was a mile away.

She pulled at his arm and he turned to her. "What is it, Bailey?"

"That's him…her," she corrected. "That's the person who kidnapped me."

"What?" Micah whipped around.

"The sneeze. I remember the sneeze. I was wearing this perfume the morning of the fashion show."

Just then, the limo driver took a turn onto the West Side Highway and took off.

"Stop the car!" Micah reached over and clamped his hand around the driver's neck. The car swerved left, then right. Horns from other cars blared as the limo veered into adjacent lanes.

Micah lunged toward the front of the car, propelling half of his upper body inside the front cabin. The car accelerated, then slowed. It lurched back and forth as Micah and the driver fought for control.

Bailey willed her limbs to move, but she was paralyzed with fear. She couldn't believe this was happening.

The car careened toward the median strip.

Bailey screamed, her body hurtling forward as the car ran aground on the shrubbery planted in the median.

"Are you okay?" Micah called from the front.

"Yes," Bailey murmured. She took inventory to make sure she wasn't telling a lie. She was pretty sure that everything was in order.

The whirl of approaching police sirens made Bailey forever grateful to the NYPD. A moment later, a uniformed officer opened the back door.

"Is everyone okay here?"

Micah kept his arm around the limo driver's neck.

"No," Bailey said. She quickly got out of the car, nearly collapsing to her knees. She pointed to the front. "The driver… I believe the driver kidnapped me."

"Ma'am?" The officer's forehead creased in a frown.

The driver's-side door opened and the limo driver tore out of the car and dashed for the northbound lanes of the West Side Highway.

"Watch out!" the officer said. He caught the driver around the waist before she could rush into the oncoming traffic.

Micah climbed out of the car and had his arms wrapped around Bailey within seconds.

"Are you okay?" he asked, gliding his hands up and down her arms and along her back.

Bailey nodded "I'm…f-fine." Her teeth were chattering and she realized her body was shivering uncontrollably, despite the coat she wore. Micah took off his wool coat and wrapped it around her.

"Can someone explain what's going on here?" the

officer barked. He continued to struggle with the limo driver, whose hat had fallen off, and whose hair lay in disarray around her head.

The driver looked up and Bailey gasped.

"Oh, my God," Bailey said.

"What's wrong?" Micah asked.

"Sasha?" She looked over at Micah. "It's Sasha Jones."

"Someone had better explain what's going on right now," the policeman warned.

"Officer, my name is Bailey Hamilton." Bailey saw the instant recognition in the man's eyes. With the way her name and picture had been splattered over the tabloids these past few months, it was hard even for those who didn't give a hoot about the fashion industry *not* to know who she was. "I believe this woman abducted me, tied me up and left me for dead in September," Bailey said.

"If I wanted you dead, I would have killed you," Sasha screamed.

Bailey gasped. She covered her mouth with her hand and recoiled at the wild-eyed hate radiating from the other woman. Bailey's entire body shook with panic.

And then came bone-melting relief.

It was over.

With her outburst, Sasha had just admitted in front of all of them that she had kidnapped Bailey. The nightmare of the past three months was truly over.

The backup the police officer had radioed in for arrived on the scene, followed several minutes later by one of the detectives who had been working with the

Hamilton family. Sasha was handcuffed and led to one of the waiting police cruisers. Once seated in the back, she started talking and could not stop. She confessed to being the one who had knocked Bailey unconscious and tied her up during Fall Fashion Week. She also confessed to slashing Kyle's tires, canceling the cake order for Zoe's wedding shower, stealing and slashing Zoe's wedding dress and all of the other mishaps that had befallen the Hamilton family over the past few months.

But she hadn't been working alone. Sasha said she had only been carrying out someone else's plans. The mastermind behind them was Jerry Prentice.

"Who's Jerry Prentice?" Micah asked.

"He owns Guava International. He's Zoe's old boss," Bailey said.

Everything began to click into place. "The Hamiltons have been a thorn in Jerry's side since he and Kyle were in design school," Sasha said. "I loved him, but he couldn't see anything past the hatred he felt for the Hamiltons. When RHD stole Zoe away, it was the last straw. Jerry orchestrated all of this! He wanted to get back at the Hamiltons. It was all Jerry."

Bailey started to explain that Zoe had left Guava International on her own, not because RHD had stolen her away from Jerry Prentice's design firm, but she realized it was useless to try to reason with someone who was obviously disturbed. And why should she waste the time? Sasha Jones was in custody, and her nightmare—her family's nightmare—was finally over.

Detective Schmidt read Sasha her rights, then instructed the officer to bring her in for booking.

"I'm going to call your father with the news," Detective Schmidt said.

"Please don't," Bailey pleaded. "Not today." She looked at Micah and then back to the detective. "Today is my brother's wedding. I don't want it ruined with this news."

"Bailey, you need to go to the hospital to get checked out," Micah said.

She shook her head. "I'm fine. I promise you, I am completely fine." He started to argue, but Bailey was adamant. "What I need to do is get to the hotel so that I can stand as bridesmaid to my future sister-in-law. We need to go now. We're running late."

As if on cue, her cell phone rang. It was Brianna's number. Bailey put a finger to her lips and stepped away from the men. She pulled in a steadying breath and answered, letting Brianna know that they had been caught up in traffic, but were on their way to the hotel.

After several more contentious minutes of arguing with both Micah and Detective Schmidt over whether or not she needed to be seen by medical professionals, Bailey hailed a cab to take them to the hotel.

They arrived an hour before the ceremony was set to start. Bailey rushed to the room where Brianna, her mother and Zoe were getting ready.

"What the heck happened?" Brianna said. "Did you get caught up in an accident?"

"You can say that," Bailey said. "I'll tell you about it later. Right now, I need to get dressed so that we can watch Kyle get hitched."

Chapter 14

The Grand Ballroom of the Childs International Hotel was the epitome of elegance, style and supreme wealth. Dazzling crystal chandeliers hung from the high ceilings, casting their bright, shimmering lights on the wedding guests seated underneath.

Burnt-orange and deep chocolate silk bunting draped from the ornate five-foot-tall candelabras that lined the wedding aisle. Each candelabra was adorned with an arrangement of fresh flowers and topped with a thick pillar candle.

Bailey stood off to the side, with Brianna right behind her. She peered into the room and couldn't help her smile when she saw Kyle, Daniel and Nelson come through a side door. Daniel and Nelson both walked to the midway point of the aisle, where they would meet up with Brianna and Bailey, and Kyle went to the front, where he would accept Zoe from her father, who was giving her away.

Bailey's eyes scanned the room and fell on Micah. He was sitting three rows from the back, on the Hamilton side. His mouth tipped up in a smile, and his eyes narrowed with heat.

"He looks as if he wants to eat you alive," Brianna said.

Bailey's skin flushed hot. Based on the way Micah's eyes seared her, she knew her sister was right.

"And I'm guessing by the look on your face that you would be just fine with that." Brianna laughed.

"Stop it," Bailey chastised with a grin.

The harpist started to play and the ceremony began.

Twenty-five minutes later, Zoe Sinclair officially became Mrs. Kyle Hamilton, and Bailey was so happy she nearly burst with it.

The minister announced them as husband and wife, and Kyle and Zoe shared a kiss that drew several murmurs of approval from the crowd. When they finally released each other, Kyle turned to the guests and said, "Now that that's out of the way, let's party."

The bridal party walked down the aisle in reverse order and went into the other side of the partitioned ballroom, where the reception was to take place. It, too, was decorated elaborately, with tall centerpieces on the round tables and floating tea lights dancing in water.

The moment the formal pictures and toast were completed, the reception turned into a full-on party. Bailey couldn't help but laugh as she watched her family living it up. Her mother and father both danced like a couple of twenty-year-olds at a nightclub.

Collin held Brianna's back to his chest as they rocked side to side, his palms splayed over her belly. If they wanted to keep their baby a secret for much longer, he would have to stop being so obvious.

Bailey didn't recognize the woman Daniel was talking to—maybe one of Zoe's cousins? She had noticed her brother dancing with her several times already tonight, and if that indulgent smile on his face was any indication, he was laying on the heavy charm.

Above all else, the most wonderful sight she'd witnessed tonight was the love that was practically pulsing between Zoe and Kyle. Zoe was glowing with it, and the way she looked at Kyle, as if he were her beginning, middle and end, had Bailey sighing with shared hope. Those two were headed toward a lifetime of happiness, and it warmed her heart to see it.

"Hey, beautiful."

Bailey jumped as Micah crept up behind her. She slapped his arm. "Thanks for scaring the living daylights out of me," she said, though she had to admit that was an exaggeration. For the first time in months, she was able to exist without a cloud of fear hovering over her.

"What is the most beautiful woman in the building doing standing here alone instead of dancing?"

"I don't know if I qualify as the most beautiful woman in the building," Bailey said. "I've got some stiff competition."

Micah shook his head. "No one even comes close."

A grin curled the corner of Bailey's mouth. "You are ridiculously sweet. You know that, don't you?"

He leaned forward and pressed a quick kiss to her lips. "So are you."

A throat cleared behind them. Bailey and Micah both turned to find Kyle and Daniel standing a few feet away.

"Oh, Lord," she muttered.

Daniel stuck his hand out to Micah. "It's about damn time."

Bailey's head reared back. "*Excuse* me?"

"I was wondering what was taking the two of you so long," Kyle said.

Micah laughed as he shared one-armed hugs with both of her brothers. Bailey wasn't sure if she wanted to hug them or hit them. She would never understand those two, ready to fight any man who dared to even look at their baby sisters one minute, accepting both Micah and Collin with open arms the next.

After Daniel and Kyle walked away, she turned to Micah and said, "I guess you have the family's stamp of approval."

"More than you know," he said.

Bailey tilted her head to the side. "What are you talking about?"

Micah gestured toward the French doors a few feet away.

"It's freezing out there," Bailey protested.

"I have ways of warming you up," he said as he urged her forward with a hand to the small of her back.

The staff at the hotel had thought of everything. There were several heat lamps radiating waves of warm air for the guests who had ventured out onto the veranda.

Micah took her by the shoulders and turned her to face him.

"Bailey, you know that I love you, don't you?"

Her heart leaped at the words. She nodded. "I do."

"I will never love another woman the way that I love you. It's just not possible. So I was hoping…" He dropped to one knee and pulled a square velvet box from his pocket. "I was hoping that you would do me the honor of becoming my wife."

Bailey covered her mouth with trembling fingers. "Oh, my goodness, Micah."

"Is that a yes?"

"Yes! Oh, my God, yes!" She threw her arms around his neck and pulled him in for a deep kiss. "Yes, I will marry you. I love you so much, Micah."

Micah cradled her face in his hands and touched her lips with the sweetest kiss Bailey had ever received in her entire life.

"I cannot wait to spend the rest of my life loving you," he whispered against her lips.

Epilogue

Micah clutched Bailey's hand in his as the credits for *Bailey Hamilton: The Face of a Franchise* rolled. The lights in the viewing room came on and the gathered crowd erupted in applause.

After viewing the documentary, the powers that be at WLNY had decided that the more serious, less sensationalized version was the perfect course of action for this story. They'd quickly entered it in a number of contests, and it had been nominated for an award at the Young African-American Directors Film Festival, which was being held in New York this year instead of Los Angeles. Bailey's entire family was in attendance, along with Micah's mother and several of his former colleagues at WLNY.

It was the perfect way to cap off what had been a harrowing month since Kyle and Zoe Hamilton's wedding.

Jerry Prentice had been arrested and slammed with a number of charges, including felony kidnapping and assault for his role in Bailey's abduction. Once taken into custody, Sasha Jones had sung like a bird, giving the police a detailed account of the plan Jerry had devised and how she'd gone about executing it. Bailey's nightmare was finally over.

Micah now suffered relentless teasing over his and Sasha's shared last name. It had become a running joke in the Hamilton family that he and Sasha were long-lost cousins. He happily endured the good-natured joking; he was willing to tolerate just about anything if it meant bringing a smile to Bailey's face.

The audience at tonight's event had been treated to a preview of the top three films in contention for the award. Micah's had been the last to be shown. When the viewings had finished, everyone had been guided to the grand ballroom where the awards banquet would be held. Once dinner had been served and enjoyed by the guests, the emcee walked up to the mic at the head table and began.

"Welcome once again to the awards banquet for the Young African-American Directors Film Festival. We support, educate and encourage upcoming talent in the film industry throughout the year, but this night is the one that we set aside to celebrate that talent and pay tribute to the stars that shine the brightest.

"You have all had the opportunity to view the top three films in the documentary category, and we are happy to announce that the winner of this year's award is Micah Jones, for his documentary *Bailey Hamilton: The Face of a Franchise.*"

Bailey yelped. The entire table stood and applauded. Micah wiped his mouth with his cloth napkin and, after kissing Bailey and then his mother, headed for the podium.

"Never in my wildest dreams could I have anticipated the turn my life would take when I first interviewed you on *Connect,*" Micah said, gazing toward Bailey. "I thought I knew what I wanted in life, but you opened my eyes to so much more."

Micah looked out at the sea of smiling faces, and with a smile of his own said, "Bailey and I are happy to announce the creation of the Bailey Hamilton Foundation for Girls, an organization that will empower young women to reach for their goals and embrace themselves for who they are."

Another round of applause sounded around the room, and Micah invited Bailey to join him at the mic.

"This woman has shown me what true courage really is, and true love. My world is complete because of her." Micah turned to her and placed a gentle kiss upon her lips. "I love you, Bailey."

"I love you, too," she said, returning his kiss with a sweet one of her own. "Thank *you* for showing me what true love is."

* * * * *

A new miniseries featuring fan-favorite authors!

The Hamiltons: Fashioned with Love
Family. Glamour. Passion.

Jacquelin Thomas	Pamela Yaye	Farrah Rochon

Styles of Seduction	*Designed by Desire*	*Runaway Attraction*
Available September 2013	*Available October 2013*	*Available November 2013*

REQUEST YOUR FREE BOOKS!

2 FREE NOVELS
PLUS 2 FREE GIFTS!

KIMANI™
ROMANCE

Love's ultimate destination!

YES! Please send me 2 FREE Harlequin® Kimani™ Romance novels and my 2 FREE gifts (gifts are worth about $10). After receiving them, if I don't wish to receive any more books, I can return the shipping statement marked "cancel." If I don't cancel, I will receive 4 brand-new novels every month and be billed just $5.19 per book in the U.S. or $5.74 per book in Canada. That's a savings of at least 20% off the cover price. It's quite a bargain! Shipping and handling is just 50¢ per book in the U.S. and 75¢ per book in Canada.* I understand that accepting the 2 free books and gifts places me under no obligation to buy anything. I can always return a shipment and cancel at any time. Even if I never buy another book, the two free books and gifts are mine to keep forever.

168/368 XDN F4XC

Name	(PLEASE PRINT)

Address	Apt. #

City	State/Prov.	Zip/Postal Code

Signature (if under 18, a parent or guardian must sign)

Mail to the **Harlequin® Reader Service:**
IN U.S.A.: P.O. Box 1867, Buffalo, NY 14240-1867
IN CANADA: P.O. Box 609, Fort Erie, Ontario L2A 5X3

Want to try two free books from another line?
Call 1-800-873-8635 or visit www.ReaderService.com.

* Terms and prices subject to change without notice. Prices do not include applicable taxes. Sales tax applicable in N.Y. Canadian residents will be charged applicable taxes. Offer not valid in Quebec. This offer is limited to one order per household. Not valid for current subscribers to Harlequin® Kimani™ Romance books. All orders subject to credit approval. Credit or debit balances in a customer's account(s) may be offset by any other outstanding balance owed by or to the customer. Please allow 4 to 6 weeks for delivery. Offer available while quantities last.

Your Privacy—The Harlequin® Reader Service is committed to protecting your privacy. Our Privacy Policy is available online at www.ReaderService.com or upon request from the Harlequin Reader Service.

We make a portion of our mailing list available to reputable third parties that offer products we believe may interest you. If you prefer that we not exchange your name with third parties, or if you wish to clarify or modify your communication preferences, please visit us at www.ReaderService.com/consumerchoice or write to us at Harlequin Reader Service Preference Service, P.O. Box 9062, Buffalo, NY 14269. Include your complete name and address.

KROM13R

Discover that Christmas wishes really do come true...

ROCHELLE ALERS
ADRIANNE BYRD
JANICE SIMS

Tragic twists of fate become the unexpected catalyst for finding peace, love and happiness during the Christmas season. As three couples experience chance encounters and unexpected reunions, they discover that their futures hold lots of happy, romantic surprises!

"Byrd writes an amazing story of sadness turning into joy."
—RT Book Reviews on *A SEASON OF MIRACLES*

Available November 2013 wherever books are sold!